An Epilogue to Innocence

Tim Baughman Jr.

CONTENTS

AUTHOR'S NOTE

The twenties are a difficult decade for young adults. It's an in-between time of life where we're just old enough to be considered responsible for ourselves, while simultaneously being just young enough to not have the experience to be fully successful with that responsibility. It is also the onset of feelings and experiences of adulthood. True love and true loss are the most common events experienced for the first time in this age range; however, the underlying themes of disease, dependency, deceit, betrayal, mental illness, suicide, and isolation loom large.

We've escaped the relative safety of childhood. While our parents, guardians, and families may still have influence on our lives, society holds the twenty-something responsible for their actions and well-being. It's an expected part of the maturation process. That does not mean, however, that the process is easy or happy. While there are certainly high points in this era of a person's life – graduating college, falling in love, workplace success, marriage, and perhaps a child all come to mind – humanity can better adapt to change if that change is one that brings success and happiness. When that change is negative is when we struggle.

The events within the stories of this book may or may not apply to you directly. We all live different lives with our own unique circumstances. But within every person's story, be that story a reality or a work of fiction, there are lessons to learn. Perhaps you'll find a character sharing a similar situation to your own. Maybe there's a complex emotion you're not sure how to handle and worry that you're the only one feeling it. My hope is that you'll find solace in this book, either through relating to the words within the pages, or through the escapism that literature provides to so many.

LJEPOTA ONI IZLUČIVATI

You could ask for two cups of sugar, and that's exactly what she'll give you. Granted, those cups of sugar may arrive in many smaller packages ranging from a teaspoon to a tablespoon, and it'll always be plain, white, granulated sugar, but she's given you sugar nevertheless. Two cups, just like you asked for.

Sometimes, her ego gets in the way of her best intentions. For every time her honor prompts her to help an old lady cross the street, there's an equal amount of vitriol delivered toward an insubordinate co-worker or an absent-minded acquaintance. If it weren't for her daily outbursts of anger, you'd begin to wonder if emotions existed inside of her at all.

Frankly, I know better. I know that she is much more giving than initially meets the eye. Likewise, I'm aware that behind every one of her outbursts is a passionate woman who wants nothing more than success, love, and freedom. All is almost exactly as you would think it'd be.

She's always been the rebel of the group, carefully disguised as the saint that public perception currently holds to be true. While she's best known for the moments where she's donating time to help stray animals find homes, she moonlights as a burlesque dancer in the homes of many friends. Night after night, she strips away the carefully pleated suits and skirts to reveal a packaging of over-moisturized olive skin that sashays across the midsections of every miscreant and lowlife in town. Oh, to be the sinner again, so as to draw the movements she makes my way once more.

Her innocence toward the harshest of life's realities became corrupted at a far earlier age than should be allowed. No human who loses a love like that ever fully recovers, regardless of what their words may say. Her breakdowns in the solitude of a bathroom stall come less frequently than they used to, though their sudden onset is still as jarring as ever, both to her as well as those around her.

I learned early on that she uses purity and professionalism to mask the depravities of the innermost desires that she possesses. While her attitude may have once been rather libertine in nature, all her mind seeks out now is stability, even if that structure doesn't come in society-approved packaging. She sits and stares out the frost-covered windows at night, hoping that the shadows of the daylight can only be caused by the brilliance of the sun. Despite what her intuition tells her, it is the very knowledge that there is an easily defined line between good and evil that keeps her going most days.

She came to me seeking shelter and opportunity. While the first emotions she revealed to me were fear and anguish, it wasn't long before the side she revealed was one of joy and optimism. Oh, that optimism -- an emotion that I have not been able to understand for quite some time now. While optimism isn't the true opposite of realism, to live solely with one but not the other is a dangerous and fruitless way to live a life. Fortunately, she and I have both recognized this and will play off each other's strengths to mask our own shortcomings.

Her greatest strength is also her greatest downfall. Human nature drives us all to succeed, however her motivations can frequently be misconstrued as selfish actions by outsiders and those who don't understand her. It's said that a mother bear is the most protective animal in the entire world, although I'm firmly convinced that anyone who says that has never met her. The number of steps that her mind tells her to take when anyone harms a person worthy of her love and affection are uncounted. The problem lies in the fact that many of those steps border on unethical at best, and her actions can be damning at their worst.

I see all these things from my distant view as an extravagant story unfolds before me. On one hand, she's won a grand war, sacrificing very little in exchange for the total and complete domination of an enemy that was never truly an opponent. Yet on the other, the foundations beneath her happiness stand as much chance of survival as matchsticks in a hurricane. It's only a matter of time before she realizes the mistake she's made and its far-reaching implications. Furthermore, it's only a matter of time before her world comes crashing down, leaving her even more alone than her most harrowing dreams could portray -- all because of the actions that she's taken.

My travels have allowed me to visit some of the most exotic and picturesque locales in the entire world. From the country sides of Ireland to the Dalmatian coastlines on the Adriatic, I've witnessed much of the finest beauty the world has to offer. I once fell in love with a beautiful woman from Portugal, only to have my love stolen away by another man who was more dashing, debonair, and financially free than myself. Beauty is fleeting, romance even more so. The only thing that can be truly counted on in this world is that the desire for revenge will be the one emotion that never leaves the table.

As I released her from our final embrace, I turned and walked away with as great of purpose in my stride as I could muster. My fear was that if I were to turn back and gaze a final time, she would turn me into a pillar of salt, as if the deluge of emotions in my mind wasn't biblical enough. I hear her voice in my dreams from time to time, the pleasant tones of her words speaking to me through a dimension I don't fully understand. She's succeeded in her mission, if only in the realm that silence has allowed.

PHOSPHOR AND FEAR

With each passing day, the memory fades away a little more. My hope is that by writing this down I can get the thought to disappear completely, since all other attempts to rid my mind of it have failed miserably.

It was just over six years ago, on a Thursday if memory serves, though it's a struggle to keep track of the days of the week anymore. My daily commute home from work was nearing its end when I received a text message. I rolled up to a red light, glancing at the screen of my phone as I came to a stop.

"Hey. I let myself in a few minutes ago. The dog is on the patio...don't let him in right away."

The text came from my then-girlfriend, Jessica. We hadn't been dating terribly long -- four or five months at most -- but considering my track record in recent years, this qualified as a long-term relationship. We'd been on the rocks for the last month or so due to trust issues both of us harbored against one another. My distrust of her stemmed from the fact that she'd slept with another man two weeks after we started dating because "she didn't realize we were actually dating". Meanwhile, Jessica's distrust of me came about because I had a female best friend who, while now married to another man, also happened to be an ex-girlfriend and one-time emergency fuck buddy.

Our latest attempt to help build a trusting relationship was a bit unconventional. We decided to trade apartments for three days. While this made both of our commutes to work longer, we each had free reign to go through the other's stuff as thoroughly as we pleased without supervision. This was day one of the experiment, and I had to head home to pack up clothes to stay at Jessica's place.

I walked from my car to the apartment door, staring into the foothills of the Rockies as I purposefully strode along the sidewalk. For a few weeks now, I'd considered moving out of Boise and finding a job somewhere warmer, though views like the one outside of my apartment complex were part of the reason I'd stayed as long as I had.

My apartment was nearly pitch black upon entry. While I knew where all of the furniture in my apartment was stationed, it was still a bit unsettling to know that all of the lights were off while someone else was inside my home, and that I didn't know specifically where that somebody was.

Logic led me to my apartment's second bedroom, from which a dim purple glow had begun emanating upon my arrival. As I strode closer to the door, a familiar tune hummed through the walls of the apartment. The song was "Aero Zeppelin" by Nirvana, the same song playing in the background when Jessica and I had sex for the first time months prior. To this day, that song is one of the few stimuli that never fails to cause my mind to have flashbacks to Jessica.

I nudged open the door to the spare bedroom, being careful not to hit the boxes I knew to be inside. Inside, I could see two black lights mounted on the walls, one on each wall perpendicular to the door. The soft glow of a laptop screen illuminated the farthest corner of the room, though it was evident that the screen had been covered with cloth.

"About time you got here," said Jessica, pulling me through the doorway and shutting the door behind us.

In the three days since I'd last seen her, Jessica had dyed her normally chestnut-brown hair a shade of platinum blonde that radiated under the black light as if it were our Earth's second sun. A bright pink streak on the right side had found its way to her lips, sticking to the shimmering lip gloss she'd decided to wear. She wore no top, her bare torso beckoning me toward her. Jessica had used the lip gloss to paint a tiny smiley face on her left breast, just inches above the nipple. Her underwear matched the pink of the streak in her hair, though the sheer lace material barely hid her body even in the unnaturally dim light.

Jessica had found my spare bed -- an air mattress I'd owned since high school – and had inflated it and placed it in the middle of the room. I could see a box of condoms, a couple pillows, a light blanket, and what looked to be a pair of dark bath towels tossed haphazardly upon the mattress. That said, it was a bit of a struggle to focus on what was on the bed with Jessica in front of me.

"I thought I was staying at your place tonight?" I asked, a coy smile forming over my face.

Jessica wrapped her arms around my neck, chuckling to herself a little as she spoke. "You are. I know that letting me have free reign of all of your stuff is a huge commitment, so I wanted to show you how much I appreciate it."

"I'm pretty sure I can figure out where this is going," I said, "but humor me and tell me what you have in mind."

Jessica's hands slid down my chest, lifting the shirttail of my button-up out of my pants. With a swift movement, she pulled the shirt over my head, tossing it carelessly behind her.

"Well," she began, "first I'm going to give you a blowjob so good that you won't be able to stand. I'm going to let you cum all over my tits and my face, and you'll be able to see every little bit of your seed thanks to these black lights."

Her hands began to unbuckle my pants, giving some breathing room to my rapidly stiffening member. She slid my trousers to the floor, her body following them down as she continued speaking.

"Once you've recovered, I'm going to drag you

over to that mattress, and I'm going to straddle your face. You're going to eat me until you get hard again. As soon as you get hard, you're going to fuck me as hard and as fast as you can until you cum again."

Jessica's hands flowed effortlessly across my body, her fingertips gently caressing my cock and making me throb more powerfully. She teasingly stuck her tongue out of her mouth, using the tip to flick at the head of my penis a few times.

"Finally, we're going to shower, clean each other up as much as we can, maybe take a little nap, and you're going to go stay at my place. Until then though, you're going to do exactly as I say."

I closed my eyes and took in the moment as I felt Jessica's steamy mouth wrap around the head of my cock. She lingered for a moment before sliding her mouth just a little down my shaft, flicking her tongue all along the way. Jessica began to move her mouth back toward the head of my dick, releasing my member with a loud popping sound as suction gave way to an absence of warmth.

Morning. October 9th, 2011. One week ago to the day. I rolled over to find my wife, Danielle, still asleep to my left. Strands of her strawberry blonde hair fluttered through the wind caused by the ceiling fan above our bed. Her breathing was calm and rhythmic, a normality for our mornings.

Our house is always quiet on Sunday mornings, though this particular morning was extra calm. A recent cold spell that had rolled through the area had prompted the birds that frequent the feeders on our porch to be less active than normal. Our cat, Lucius, had even taken to the thought of a silent morning, passing out across the arm of my recliner in the glow of the rising sun. Not even the sound of pouring food into his feeding dish prompted Lucius' movement, though he did open his eyes and acknowledge my existence.

I poured myself a glass of orange juice and grabbed a granola bar out of the cabinet, heading over to the couch to enjoy the silence. I'm not much for a silent home, honestly. If I had my way, there would always be music softly playing wherever I walked. Ambient sound helps me think clearly, while silence causes my mind to fall into thought patterns that I typically find unpleasing. This morning though, I wanted the silence. I needed time to reflect on my dream from the night prior.

It had been four or five months since I had last dreamed about my final encounter with Jessica. With each passing occurrence, the memory becomes less full and clear, though it's not going away fast enough for my liking. While that day was bar-none the greatest sexual experience of my life, it is also a day I'd prefer to wipe from my mind for the rest of eternity.

After our romp in my old place, I showered and left to go stay at Jessica's apartment. That night, around two in the morning, I got a phone call from the police asking me to return home. A neighbor had called the cops due to the sound of a gunshot echoing throughout the neighborhood. When they arrived, the police found Jessica collapsed in my second bedroom, blood splattered on the wall behind her head and a .38 Special on the ground beside her. The coroner ruled her death a suicide, though Jessica never left a note as to why she took her own life.

Six months later, I went on my first date with Danielle, who also happens to be the local coroner. Normally when you meet your future wife, it isn't at three in the morning at a crime scene where she's inspecting your ex-girlfriend's dead body. Yet, fate thought it would be an interesting way to transition my life from the rockiest relationship I'd ever experienced to the most stable one.

Danielle and I married two years to the day after our first date. Our honeymoon was a three-week excursion across the coasts of Italy and France, just as she wished to do from her childhood. Ten months later, we moved into the small house that we currently reside in. Danielle chose the house partly because of its cozy front porch, but mostly due to its proximity to her job. My commute tripled in length thanks to the move, though it was important to make Danielle's life as stress free as possible.

At Danielle's prompting, I've been seeing a psychologist recently. My father unexpectedly died a year ago, and while I feel I'm over his passing, Danielle's wholehearted disagreement swayed me into seeing a professional. Within weeks, the psychologist agreed with me in saying that for the most part, I had moved on from my dad's sudden death. Instead, the psychologist attributes my melancholy attitude toward life to dissatisfaction with my marriage -- more specifically, to the fact that it's a very one-sided relationship.

October 8th, 2011 was Danielle's birthday, her 33rd to be exact. That morning, Danielle woke me up to tell me she wanted two things for her birthday -- dinner at her favorite restaurant, and sex at her workplace. Dinner was easy enough, as I'd booked reservations at the restaurant three weeks prior knowing full well that she'd likely want to eat there. As for workplace sex, I'm game for most anything, though admittedly fucking in a morgue isn't my ideal rendezvous point. Still, that's what I did. I love my wife and want to make her happy.

I've asked for little things like that in the past. Once the request was that Danielle would dress like a schoolgirl. Another time I wanted handcuffed to the bed. Yet another involved getting her to wear lingerie I'd purchased for our honeymoon. It wasn't like I was asking her to bring a friend over for a threesome (though, as is the case with nearly every human, the thought of group sex did sound alluring from time to time), or even to do anything out of her comfort zone. All I wanted was something to be done with my interests and desires in mind.

Subconsciously, I know why I'm dreaming of Jessica. Despite all of the fighting and bickering we had between us, Jessica appreciated my desire to always put my partner first in life. She often paid me back in kind, be it by surprising me with dinner, or by planning a tantalizing sexual experience just as she did with the black light night.

Doing things for others isn't Danielle's strong suit. There were times when we were dating where she paid for dinner unexpectedly, or where she came to my apartment to stay with me without my prompting. I've learned though with Danielle that work comes first, her desires come second, and whatever time is left over is equally devoted to the first two items on that list.

At the present, I find that I just want this period of time to pass. The psychologist said that a great way for me to get past my preoccupation with my own gratification is to write out what I'm thinking. The exercise is supposed to help me determine if the thoughts going through my mind are just a passing phase fueled by the lack of any sexual interaction, or if there's a deeper ingrained desire in my mind not being fulfilled.

If the thoughts disappear after I write, I just need to ask Danielle for more sex, or for her to initiate it more often. If there is a deeper ingrained issue, at that point I need to figure out what that issue is. I completely hope that there is a separate issue here besides the sex. I know Danielle will have no desire to fix our intimate relationship. What Danielle wants, Danielle gets...and nothing else until then.

It's likely a bit unfair of me to characterize Danielle as someone with no sexual desire for her husband. At times, it's quite the contrary. It's during those times that she makes promises to me, often times calling back to previous requests I've made of her and telling me that those desires will come true soon. Of course, that's the last time we discuss my desires, and if I bring up the subject again, Danielle yells at me to quit pressuring her, after which I end up apologizing repeatedly for my behavior.

Our basement has a room in the back that I've turned into my personal office. Danielle rarely bothers me if I'm in there. She says it's because she hates being in the basement more than she has to be, though I'm fairly sure she just has no interests in messing with my office. I'll occasionally use the room to work from home, and fortunately those days are happening more and more. It is peaceful to be able to get work done without having others bother you.

A lamp in the far corner of the room, as well as a small lamp on the corner of my desk light the office. The lamp in the corner is tall, housing three bulbs that fill the room with a brilliant white light that keeps me awake during sleepy mornings. That light is my day-to-day source of illumination, the light that allows me to work. At the moment, I've turned on the desk lamp, which dimly fills the room with the soft glow of a black light.

Today, I learned that like semen and glitter-filled lip gloss, tears also have a bit of fluorescence under a black light. While the shine isn't the same brightness, there's a definite faint glow tears produce. With a deep breath and an extended sigh, I put down my pen and head off to the store. I have a few purchases to make before the light goes out for good.

A DELAYED FIRST DATE

Paul Akselsen. Paul Fucking Akselsen. After thirteen years of trying, Paul Akselsen and I are on a date.

I first met Paul when my family moved from Chicago to Rapid City, South Dakota. I was 15 years old at the time, my mind filled with struggles caused by some combination of my parents' sudden decision to move, general existential teen angst, and the culture shock of moving from a city of over 2 million people to one in the neighborhood of 60,000. I lived in a suburb with more people than that, so I was less than thrilled with the move. Until I met Paul.

I met him at the homecoming dance that fall. I didn't have a date, so I went with my first friend at the new school -- and still my best friend -- Kenzie, and her then-boyfriend...whose name eludes me at the moment. Brian, maybe? Ben? Brad? The hell if I know. We were there less than an hour when Paul walked in with his date. He looked fantastic in his navy blue suit, a simple orange tie providing a contrasting pop immediately drew my eyes up his chest and to his gorgeous face.

While a jaw chiseled from the finest granite was his most noticeable feature, my eyes wandered to other parts of that wonderful face. Paul's brilliant white teeth glistened in the dimly lit gymnasium, their radiance giving off a heavenly glow that was bright enough to land an airplane. His blonde hair was a bit longer than most boys kept their hair – just long enough to be dangerous, yet not long enough to be mistaken as feminine. With every look, his alluring brown eyes alternated screaming "I want to do kinky things to you and your twin sister" and "your mother will love me because I don't curse in public".

I got Kenzie's attention away from sucking face with Chris/Kyle/Frank/whatever by tugging on her orange-red hair and pulling her toward me. I pointed her face in Paul's direction to gaze upon the same thing I was seeing.

"Who is THAT?" I asked, trying to hush my excitement as much as I could in the crowded room.

"That's Paul Akselsen," Kenzie answered. "I have biology with him. And the girl on his arm is his girlfriend, Michelle Peterson."

"Wait, you have class with him?" I was overjoyed that someone I know actually knows this heaven-sent man. "Can you introduce him to me? Please?"

"I'm not sure that's a good idea, Hela. He has a girlfriend."

Of course he had a girlfriend. He's Paul Fucking Akselsen. He is the Lord's gift to my eyesight, my dreams, and (that same Lord willing) any other part of me he wanted to gift himself to.

I gave up that night. I don't know if it was nerves or Paul's aura that overwhelmed me, but I wasn't able to bring myself to pursue things any further that day. I couldn't stop thinking about him. Paul Akselsen consumed me. I lived for the day he'd be single and I could win his heart – and for the day I could feel him against me, his hard chest pressed to mine, our breathing strained and our faces flushed. I think I would have killed for just one date.

Paul's dating status didn't change much throughout high school. While his relationship with Michelle didn't last past the end of that fall, he dated numerous other girls -- none for more than a few months at a time -- through our graduation. I had two boyfriends during that same time, though I never took either of them seriously.

It wasn't like there was anything wrong with them either. I've heard that one of them is now working for NASA, while the other is an investment banker on Wall Street. They just...they weren't Paul.

When college came around, Paul and I went our separate ways. Paul was the captain of the school's wrestling team and was good enough to get a scholarship at Oklahoma State. While I admit I secretly looked into following him there, my mother's connections to her alma mater, Valparaiso

University, got me free admission. Free college made moving back to Northern Indiana an easy decision. Kenzie's mom died three weeks into senior year, so instead of coming to Valpo with me as she had originally planned, she stayed close to home and went to NAU in Rapid City.

Over the next three years, I started to forget about Paul. Yes, he'd creep up in my mind whenever I'd hear someone (particularly ESPN) mention Oklahoma State. Yes, I'd think about him on occasion if Kenzie brought him up in conversation. And yes, just like in high school, he was a part of at least 40% of my masturbatory fantasies. However, by the end of my junior year of college, I could honestly say that for the first time since high school that Paul wasn't my main male focus.

I have Derek Lawson to thank for that. We met at a party just off campus during finals week in the fall semester of my junior year. He was one of the nicest people I'd ever met. We hit it off over a game of beer pong, talked to each other a few times a week before going on our first date that spring, and have been together ever since. Five months ago, Derek proposed to me, making me the "happiest woman in the world". It sounds cliché, but it's the truth.

Despite our long relationship, Derek had never met Kenzie. The trip from Indiana to South Dakota was far more than I generally liked to travel in college, and after graduating, I'd stayed in Valparaiso. I didn't venture back to South Dakota for holidays, as my parents would fly to Chicago so that we could all have

Christmas/Thanksgiving/Easter with my grandparents. For Kenzie's part, she stayed living with her dad and her four younger siblings after college. She'd flown to Valpo twice to see me, but had never crossed paths with Derek.

After months of planning, I finally found a time where Derek and I could fly to Rapid City to see my family. More importantly, Kenzie could finally meet my fiancée. Our plan was to have dinner with Kenzie after spending a few days with my family.

Thursday night rolled around quicker than I expected. Derek was excited to meet Kenzie, and I was thrilled to be able to see my best friend again for the first time in quite some time. I wasn't even concerned whether or not Derek and Kenzie would get along...I already knew they would.

Derek and I arrived at the restaurant first, our waiter leading us to our reserved table. We'd only been seated a few moments when I got a text from Kenzie.

"Hey. Omw now. Just picked up my date. It's a first date and I'm nervous. Sorry I didn't give you more of a heads up. Be there soon"

I giggled uncontrollably to myself.

"What's going on?" Derek asked.

"Kenzie's bringing a date!" I responded, my voice squeaking a little from excitement. "She hasn't dated much since high school, so this could be really big for her."

"So I suppose I should be on my best behavior?"

"You already will be because you love me."

Derek and I sat for a few minutes, sipping at our glasses of water. As I idly commented on something related to my family, I felt a familiar pair of arms wrap around my shoulders and hug tightly.

"I fucking missed you," Kenzie whispered into my ear.

"I know you did," I responded quietly without turning.

Kenzie came whipping around in front of me, her forest green dress rippling as she moved. Her smile revealed true excitement; however, her eyes were full of nervousness – clearly for her date. She reached out, grabbing her date's hand and pulling him into view.

"Hela, Derek, this is my date, Paul."

...Paul Akselsen. Does Kenzie even remember my little obsession with him? It was so long ago...and it doesn't even matter. After thirteen years of waiting, I'm on a date with Paul Akselsen. Never mind the fact that he's technically Kenzie's date. Never mind the fact that my fiancée is sitting twelve inches to my right. Never mind that I'll be getting married in nine months. I'm on a date with Paul Motherfucking Akselsen.

How the hell did Kenzie manage to go on a date with him? How isn't he married already? Wait...that's stupid. I'm so dumb. There is no way

Paul Akselsen would ever get married. He's too damn good looking to get married. Men like that don't just marry. They age like fine wine and divorce twice by the age of 34, only to receive child support checks from their ex-wives even though they don't have kids. And you know why they get those checks, because like them, their sperm are just that good looking.

Of all of the times for Paul Akselsen to show up, it HAD to be now when both Derek and Kenzie are here. If I made a move on Paul now, not only would I alienate my fiancée, I'd crush the relationship with my best friend. I'd take the two surest things in my life and destroy them just like that. Then again, maybe the two of them would be up for a foursome. I know Paul's in. When you look like that, group sex is your standard Thursday night activity, which is of course preceded by Wednesday night hot yoga and pool, Tuesday night Kama Sutra practice while reading Shakespeare, Mon...

"EARTH TO HELA!" Kenzie shouted.

I snapped out of my trance, only to realize that Kenzie and Paul had taken their seats across from me. All the while, I'd been staring at the space that Paul had occupied when Kenzie started talking. I felt like a damned fool.

In spite of my momentary lapse of focus, dinner went off reasonably well. Kenzie and Derek hit it off just as I expected they would. When Kenzie and I talked, it was as if my long-lost sibling and I had reconnected without a missed day. Paul was magnificently talented in how he balanced his conversations of rather dull and boring topics with

Derek against the witty and cultured conversations he held with Kenzie.

As for me...well...I couldn't bring myself to say anything to Paul all night. He seemed content not to engage me in discussion directly, almost as if my presence unsettled him somehow. If he knew how hard I'd fuck Derek later that night while thinking about him, I'm sure he'd either be more or less unsettled, though I don't particularly know which. Despite the total silence between us, this was a date with both Paul and I present. It wasn't just any first date. It was OUR first date.

It was perfect.

SOMA

Thanks to studies conducted by Tulane University in 2017 and confirmed by the University of Oregon, Uppsala University, and the University of South Australia in 2024, it is an accepted scientific fact that there are an infinite number of universes parallel to the one in which our consciousness resides. While infinity may be a concept that humanity is unlikely to understand at any point in the near future, I present to you an idea that has been in existence for as long as man himself.

One.

One is the great equalizer in the world of mathematics. On either side of the concept of nothingness, one provides the world with a logical starting point for reaching all entities beyond its existence. One conscious mind is all that a normal person can perceive. Even those locked away in our darkest asylums who can see more than their single being are often taken to be so deranged that the world, along with both the good and bad within it, have shunned them away. One represents normality, order, monogamy, life, beginnings, endings, and all that is right within the physical and psychological confines of our very beings.

One.

My daughter turned one year old yesterday. Her name is Alma and she is a beautiful little girl. Alma inherited my blonde locks and defined cheekbones, though that's all the more she really takes after me physically. While she doesn't speak much, I was fortunate enough for the first words out of Alma's mouth to be "dada," just as I had secretly hoped they would be during the entire time leading up to her birth. It's such a simple word - dada - yet a word that carries so much weight when it leaves the mouth of a child, its intonations fluttering gently through space and time before landing within the ears of that same child's awaiting parents. That is, if all goes as planned.

One.

That's how many parents my dear Alma has. One year ago today, just one day after she gave birth to our little Alma, I lost my Soma. All of the things that give beauty to the world were personified by Soma's existence. Her chestnut-brown hair flowed across her shoulders with delicate waves that mirrored those found in the rippling streams of backwoods Idaho. Her jade green irises twinkled with a passion for life so rarely seen in the soul of anyone but a child. Her flawless fair skin (a 6 on the Von Luschan scale) was reminiscent of a simpler time in her life; a time where her skin, eyes, and hair were all filled with vigor and enthusiasm.

One.

Soma's lip ring was her singular visible link between the harsh reality of her death and the joyous nature of our first meeting. For as casual as she looked from the neck up -- her hair twisted up in a messy bun, highlighting her exquisite face - her attire from the neck down was equally as sophisticated. She wore an elegant knee-length red dress made from a fine chiffon, a singular strap across her right shoulder holding it to her exquisite silhouette. She clutched a small silver handbag in her glove-covered hands, the sleeve of the gloves running well past her elbows and drawing me immediately back to her splendid face, all the while seducing me into her hypnotic aura.

One.

A lone doctor visited me less than 24 hours after Alma's birth to tell me that Soma had passed on from this world. His name eludes me at the moment...Rohen or Roenick I think it was...much of the encounter has since become blurred in my mind. He strode out to the waiting room, his cautious gait giving away the awful news before he'd uttered a single word. My gut tells me there was crying, shouting, pain, and suffering all pouring out from me when the doctor gave me the news, though I couldn't tell you anything beyond that. Excluding moments together with my darling Alma, I don't remember most of the next four months. My mother and father stopped hearing from me, and while I know my sister, Roslyn, came to care for Alma many nights, I don't recall interacting with her during that time.

One.

In binary logic, there are but two possible symbols: one and zero. Everything in the binary world is black and white, with not a solitary marker to provide a point of the in-between. I was told at a young age of a supposed worldly concept that functioned in a similar manner to binary logic. That logic has a name of karma, a destiny or fate brought on a person because of his or her own actions. No matter how much the world got you down, karma would lift you back up if you were a great person. If you were an awful human being, you may have successes, but karma would be certain that those triumphs would be paid back with pain in triplicate.

One.

A solitary night jarred my memory back into existence. Much like other nights, I awoke to the sounds of Alma crying in her crib, the pangs of hunger awakening her from slumber. I produced a bottle of formula from the refrigerator, warmed it to an acceptable temperature, and proceeded to feed it to my daughter until she drifted back off to sleep. I laid her down in her crib, sitting in the rocking chair I'd placed at the crib's foot so that I could watch Alma rest. I quietly told Alma that I love her, and that her mommy Soma loves her too. I then too descended into slumber, only to snap back into consciousness during a dream that seemed all too real.

One.

When she was alive, one of Soma's favorite activities was to drive out to the state park, find the most isolated hiking trail that she could, and take a long walk by herself. It freed her mind, she said, allowing her to function in the world around her. Soma worked by day as an oncologist for a local hospital, spending much of her time administering radiation therapy and chemotherapy to people whom she likely would live longer than. Soma found the good of the world in everyone, most notably in me, and in the news of our coming child. Being a mother was Soma's great reward for the hours she put toward trying to help others live just a little bit longer in their own lives.

One.

I found myself (albeit in a dream) walking down one of those isolated hiking trails that Soma so loved to frequent when she needed to clear her mind. I saw her walking toward me, her radiant smile beaming with her never-ending love for me. Soon, the trail would turn to the unfinished baby room of our apartment, the room set just as it was two days prior to Alma's birth -- the last day that Soma saw the nursery. As she got closer to me, I would extend my arms, reaching desperately for one final opportunity to feel her embrace, only for Soma to fade into the forest behind her.

One.

Statistically speaking, roughly one out of every 6,500 expectant mothers in the United States in the year 2026 died at childbirth. Soma wasn't the only mom to not make it home with her child...but she was the only one I cared about. Every day, I think about the multiverse concept, knowing that somewhere in a parallel universe Soma, Alma, and I are a beautiful family celebrating Alma's first birthday. Roslyn and my parents are around, taking pictures of my lovely little girl as she sits on her mother's lap, both of them beaming with joy throughout it all.

One.

But do you know how many universes my mind can comprehend? One. That one universe -- that miserable, desolate fucking existence of a universe -- is the one where I don't have the woman who I was meant to spend the rest of my life with. There must be universes where Soma and I never met, universes where we couldn't make it through our seventeen-month courtship, universes where we broke off the engagement, and likely still others where we divorced or fell apart well before she ever became pregnant. Statistics, science, and common knowledge say that's the case. I can't see those places. All I see is this universe.

One.

One goddamn life that I have to live without the partner that I deserve. One child in my poor, dear Alma who won't understand why she doesn't have a mommy when all the other kids at school do. Even if I do manage to remarry (a concept I find obscene, though Roslyn is insistent I will find love again), that woman won't be Alma's mommy. It won't be her mommy. Do you realize how difficult it'll be to explain that to her? How the fuck does the world expect me to comprehend the concept of an infinite multiverse when I can't even figure out how in the hell I will tell my own daughter that she'll never get to meet her mother in any form other than pictures and a tombstone?

One.

If there was one person in the entire world who deserved everything great in life, it was Soma. There is no level of karmic balance that you can show me in the world that will ever convince me that Soma's death is justifiable. I hate the fact that I was powerless to stop her from dying. I hate that I couldn't take her place in some way. I hate that I miss her every waking moment of the day and twice so at night.

One.

Everyone tells me that there is one thing that will endure past all of this -- past all of the pain, the suffering, the anger, the anguish, past the tears and the heartache and the loneliness I live with every moment of every minute of every day. They tell me that the one thing that will endure will be the memories of our time together. I'll remember that gorgeous red dress she wore when we first met. I'll remember the first time we had sex, our bodies collapsing in a melded mass of intertwined flesh, sweat, and smiles. I'll remember when she said yes to me, and the immediate release of butterflies from my stomach when I popped up from my knees into her waiting embrace. I'll remember our wedding day and the immaculate, flawless vision she was as she walked down the aisle with me for the first time as my wife. That's what I've been told I'll remember.

That's not what I remember.

Do you want to know what I remember? I remember a faceless, nameless doctor walking through a hospital waiting room to tell me my wife was dead. I remember seeing her sickly corpse, her once beautiful skin completely devoid of color and of all the vigor I once knew, leaving my mind to know nothing but that she was gone. I remember the flickers of light off her silver lip ring, taunting me with the hope that her bluing lips would spring back to life, and that everything would have been a joke. A giant, tasteless, soulless joke where my fucking wife isn't actually dead.

I remember her funeral, when a procession of grieving friends and family walked by me, wishing their condolences to me. I remember collapsing to the ground, sobbing with all the energy I could muster as her casket was lowered into the ground. The sounds of the dirt being shoveled to fill up her burial plot still haunt my dreams at night. I had to have laid on the ground for half an hour before people kept telling me we needed to go.

Why the fuck would I want to go? Why would I leave the woman who changed everything in my life for the better, even as the nightfall of her death became painfully visible around me? You try losing happiness, losing hope, losing love, and then tell me that you want to leave. Just try it. Try it one fucking time and tell me that you're a stronger man than I am. Fucking do it.

One.

My daughter turned one year old yesterday. On that same day, she said her first word that wasn't the same syllable over and over. No mama, no dada, no papa (as she's learned to refer to my father). It was a different word. It was a word that I'd uttered so many times as I fell asleep every night, and a word that Alma heard herself every time she fell asleep from the day I first brought her home.

"So-ma." she said.

I miss her too, sweetie. I really do.

ELK RIDGE

I watched today as the final Elk Ridge Coffee met its demise at the hands of a steel wrecking ball. It was the last remnant of a quieter time here in Baldwin, a time filled with fewer stresses in spite of an equal (if not greater) number of distractions in my life. The window from my office overlooking Roper Road allowed me a front row seat to the destruction of the thirty-eight-year-old building, its bricks crumbling to the ground as the wrecking ball powered through wall after wall. The building itself came down in less than two hours, with most of the debris cleanup being completed by the end of the day. It was all so simple, brutal, and efficient.

Despite having a thirty-second walk to the now demolished Elk Ridge Coffee, I had not been to that location or any other for over five years. At one time, Elk Ridge Coffee was a growing local establishment, its first location founded in 1958 a mere six blocks away from my apartment on Clemens Avenue. Its second and third locations sprung up in the fall of 1975, including a shop on Riverwalk Lane mere minutes from my home, as well as the Roper Road location. By the early 1990s, Elk Ridge Coffee had twenty-six locations in seventeen cities, including five in Baldwin. The chain would hit its peak in 1997, with its owner Charles Hanlan opening a thirty-second location before selling the chain to Peter Church, a real estate broker who had recently moved to the area from San Bernadino, California.

While Elk Ridge Coffee expanded swiftly under Hanlan's leadership, perhaps the most endearing fact about the place was that Hanlan had created an environment that was inviting and accepting of all people. It wasn't uncommon to see patrons of Elk Ridge, both young and old, sit around at the shop's tables and sip coffee while playing cards and talking. Refills of coffee came at a third of the cup's full price, while the cards and chit-chat came at no cost.

Church decided that the best way for Elk Ridge to remain profitable as it expanded was to increase foot traffic in every shop. Though his plan certainly would drive the customer count up, Church's aggressive marketing tactics alienated some of the chain's existing client base. While the plan was initially successful, Church's move to have all breakfast foods served at the shop come prepackaged rather than be made in-house was the initial stimulus for the company's downturn. Elk Ridge never opened a new store under Church's leadership. Three stores shut down in his first year leading the company, with the total shop count dwindling to nineteen by 2007.

It was in 2007 that Natasha began working at the Elk Ridge Coffee on Riverwalk Lane. She started as a part-time employee in May of that year, only taking a job at the shop after losing her job as an actuary the prior December. By the end of the year, Natasha was a full-time employee, and was offered an assistant manager role at the original Clemens Avenue location just after Valentine's Day in 2008. Unfortunately for Natasha, the Clemens Avenue location was one of eleven Elk Ridge stores shut down by Church in 2008. With the store's closure in June, it was a foregone conclusion in Natasha's mind that she would yet again be unemployed.

For what he lacked in traditional business acumen, Church was an equally impressive salesman, gladhander, and HR professional. With every Elk Ridge location that closed down in 2008, Church was personally on site to oversee the final day of the store's operation. He collected information from each and every employee, then passed it along to local temp agencies to attempt to alleviate any amount of unemployment time for former Elk Ridge Coffee employees. Church touted that not a single one of the ex-Elk Ridge employees was out of a job longer than three months after a store closed down, but his claims are widely disputed by those who actually lost their jobs.

As the last employees filed out of the now-closed Clemens Avenue location, Church turned to Natasha, handing her an offer letter to be his new personal assistant. The job would pay nearly double what she was making as a manager, taking care of all of her financial needs and then some. That same night, Natasha took all her friends out for drinks in celebration, including her college roommate Kaitlyn, whom I was dating at the time. Natasha was vibrant and full of life, her mind excitedly racing with scenarios of how the extra money would help her get out of her tiny apartment and into a small house where she could park her car in a driveway without the worry of yet another parking ticket.

There were ten of us at dinner that night – Natasha, Kaitlyn, myself, Amber (Kaitlyn's younger sister), three friends from Natasha's college art club, Devon (my roommate), and Mike and Lea James (Amber's newly married roommates). Despite the oldest of us (Devon) being just shy of 30 and all without kids, the echoes of "congratulations Mom" rang throughout the bar. To nearly everyone who knew her, Natasha was mom. She was the one who routinely held Kaitlyn's hair back as she threw up after a long night of drinking. She was the one who scheduled all the art club meetings and gave them meaning. She was even the occasional chauffeur for young Amber in high school, including to prom, as a way to avoid the embarrassment of being taken to prom by your mother (as Amber so delicately put it).

Though I hadn't known her long, I knew that Natasha craved responsibility. She wanted people to give her more than she could handle. Natasha knew exactly where her breaking point was, yet loved challenging it. Her mentality screamed athlete, stockbroker, or elite salesperson. She was driven to succeed, and yet never wanted her success to overshadow the things she did for others. Kaitlyn saw Natasha as her protector; as the big sister she never had.

I found out much later that Natasha's need to protect and succeed was driven by a childhood accident. One summer, Natasha was playing baseball with her younger sister, Morgan, a few cousins, and some other kids around the neighborhood. While Natasha enjoyed playing baseball, she was an average player, usually getting picked near the end of those playing. Morgan, on the other hand, was exceptionally athletic and a particularly good pitcher both baseball and softball style. Her repeated practice with her older cousins had left her miles ahead of girls her own age, meaning she was usually the first person picked, regardless of gender.

Morgan threw a pitch to one of the neighborhood boys during a game that day. He was a fairly strong boy and was two years older than most of the group (which gave him five years on Morgan). The combination of the boy's strength, quick hands, and an errant pitch by Morgan spelled disaster. The ball recoiled off of the bat, hitting Morgan directly in the face. She crumpled to the ground in a heap, screaming a high-pitched wail of terror that paralyzed Natasha with fear. While everyone else ran to get adults or look at Morgan, Natasha couldn't move her body. Instead she stood at third base, her legs pinned to the ground in terror as her eyes released tears in rivers.

Morgan lost sight in her left eye from the injury. She took her own life three years later from the chronic pain that had never relented after the incident. According to Kaitlyn, on that same night we went out to celebrate Natasha's success, Natasha ended the night by laying in her bed and telling

Morgan about her day. Just as she had every day since Morgan died.

I've never lost a family member, especially not one so close to my own age as Morgan was to Natasha. Had Kaitlyn not told me about what happened to Morgan, the existence of Natasha's previous hardships never would have crossed my mind. Yet knowing that part of her past, that dark, depressing moment in Natasha's life, humanized her actions to me somewhat. Instead of being our group's mother-like figure because she liked having control (which may have still been true to some extent), it was a reflection on her desire to protect others where she had failed previously. All her hard work to reach success in her professional life was no longer the traits of a workaholic, but now it depicted itself as a drive to always keep moving forward, if only to bury the memory of the one day when she couldn't move.

Natasha's first day on the job as Peter Church's assistant would also be her last. She was tasked with cleaning out the Clemens Avenue location, returning all of the Elk Ridge Coffee memorabilia to the chain's now-main location on Roper Road. As she cleaned, Church attacked her from behind, using his large frame to overpower and sexually assault Natasha. Court records note that she was able to flee from Church before he raped her, however in her hurry to leave the building, she tripped over a table leg, her head crashing into a corner of the shop's front wall.

When firefighters arrived on the scene at the smoldering remains of the Clemens Avenue store, just after 1:20 p.m., they found Natasha's charred remains soaked in gasoline residue, and covered with wood and paper ash. Peter Church went on trial for Natasha's murder, but the jury found that there was not enough evidence to convict Church of her death, nor of arson of the store. In the research process, investigators were able to find that Church had been secretly funneling profits from Elk Ridge Coffee to his real estate firm, all while buying up land in Ecuador for development. Church ultimately plead guilty to tax evasion and to providing safe haven to Ecuadorian drug lords, though he committed suicide in prison before his sentencing.

I always found it to be a bit of a shame that Peter Church ended his own life. For many, suicide is seen as an escape from pain that never ceases. I have to imagine that's how Morgan felt – free from pain. She was free from a torturous life that she had no control over. A pain and a hurt that starts when you least expect it and that you can't control is heartbreaking. Morgan's actions seem justified, if only slightly. On the other hand, to see someone like Church use suicide as an escape from retribution for his actions seems unfair. To destroy a life is one matter, but to do so without paying penance for your wrongdoing is depressing.

Charles Hanlan took back over the remaining eight Elk Ridge Coffee stores in late 2008, though he quickly began closing them down. Patrons reported seeing a gruesome looking spirit walking from table to table throughout the day, its head and face melted in an unrecognizable mass. While the spirit largely just went about its own business, many customers would notice that tables would be cleaned up without the actual employees doing so.

Every day at 1:20 p.m., clocks would stop working inside Elk Ridge Coffee locations, and all hot drinks in the building would instantly turn cold.

I was a witness to this spirit myself in my final visit to Elk Ridge Coffee. After leaving the office one winter evening in 2008, I crossed the street to buy a hot cocoa from the Roper Road Elk Ridge location. A man and his wife were in line in front of me, arguing about whether to buy a beach house in California or North Carolina. The man sternly decided that their purchase would be in California, shouting at his wife as the barista handed him his iced coffee. As the man finished taking the drink from the barista it burst into flames, engulfing his entire arm within seconds. A shrill sound of a female's voice boomed throughout the establishment, its refrain equal parts crying and laughing.

As the demolition crew left the Roper Road site, I stared out at the shop's remains, realizing that even though this was the symbolic end to the Elk Ridge Coffee chain, its spirit had died long ago. A blue taxi pulled up to the front door of our office building, letting an older gentleman and his wife out onto the sidewalk. Just as the car started to pull away, the driver slammed on his brakes, coming to a complete stop in the middle of the road. I watched as a blue-auraed spirit climbed out of the rubble of the store, taking care to grab a coat from the one remaining wall of the shop, then strode across the street to the waiting taxi.

From the car, a second spirit exited. A young girl, perhaps fourteen or fifteen years in age stepped out from the door, and excitedly leaped into the air. The two shared a warm, lengthy embrace, punctuated by the first spirit burying her head in the shoulder of her counterpart and sobbing. It had been years since Morgan and Natasha had seen each other, but in their moment of reuniting, time apart vanished like steam from a hot coffee cup into the cool winter air.

Natasha and Morgan ended their hug, and readied themselves to leave. Morgan bounded into the car, her energy filled with a youthful enthusiasm she must have shown during her life. Natasha was more deliberate, taking the time to look around her and observe the scenery. Natasha looked up at my office window -- her smiling face just as excited as it had been that night in 2008. She gave a brief wave with her hand, then entered the car and shut the door.

THE STRONGEST FEELINGS ARE ON THE INSIDE

Joy

Ding-ding. Ding-ding. Ding-ding.

Three in the morning is a hell of a time for anyone to be doing anything. Believe you me, under normal circumstances I wouldn't dream of being awake at this godforsaken hour. Taxi cab drivers won't take calls for less than $20 at this time of night, and if you hope to score a hooker from the Barnes-Grotto District, you'd better hand that lady of the night two of Ben Franklin's smiling faces (at minimum).

It hasn't always been this way, you know. I used to enjoy the night. The solitude of night from the rest of the world brought me comfort that is difficult to replicate. While the majority of people use the night to sleep away the worries of the day, I once allotted the darkest part of the day to recharge without resting. Often, I'd find myself laying on the roof of my apartment building (at least on the nights I didn't work), staring off into space (quite literally) as the sounds of a sleeping town passed by beneath me. One night a duck landed on the roof beside me. I shared my popcorn with him.

In the fall of 2005, I quit my job as a security guard, opting to take a position that had better pay and benefits. The downside to working at a library is not the near silence that you maintain throughout the day, nor is it the fact that the typical person you're interacting with is either 8 or 80 (with very few cases of a middling option). My biggest struggle was the hours. Working hours that mirror those of most business places don't mesh well with my internal body clock, nor have they for the last 10 years since I started at the library.

Most days, any location within Chesterland County is a quiet place. During my time as a security guard, I spent more time chasing off stray dogs who tried climbing into dumpsters than I did worrying about whether or not someone would break into the store I was watching. Such is life in a county with a population of around 50,000 people. It's an area just large enough to have a strip club, a few hookers, and mild crime threats, but still small enough that the police don't feel the need to actively try to shut any of the aforementioned items down, in spite of protests from local "religious" groups.

My library branch -- the Chesterland County Central Branch -- is by far the largest of the seven branches spread out across the county. As of January 2014, we had nearly 4,500 books and magazines on our shelves, with nearly double that number available as ebooks for loan. The elderly folk who come into the library tell me there's something comforting about the smell of a paper book, and I tend to agree. After all, paper books remind me of a time where I didn't have electricity or running water, so I draw a certain level of comfort knowing that my life isn't like that anymore.

Ding-ding. Ding-ding. Ding-ding.

You know what makes a completely dark room way too bright at three in the morning? The light from a cell phone screen. I'm not one to typically complain about electronically manufactured light in a dark room. After all, I refuse to watch TV unless all other lights are off in my living room, and only then if my blackout curtains have been drawn to make sure there won't be any sort of glare on the screen. But cell phones -- those indispensable little bastards that 97% of Americans over the age of 11 seem to possess -- have a vendetta against my eyes if the lights are off.

My phone specifically has been lighting up constantly for the last seven hours or so. Roughly every five to fifteen minutes, I'll get a new text or call from someone. The phone proceeds to light up my bedroom with sun-like brightness as it plays its familiar refrain. Ding-ding. Ding-ding. Ding-ding. I could put the phone on silent and turn it over, though it's not like I'd be able to sleep anyway. Happiness is confusing like that.

I met Tori during my second week at the library. Her first words to me were "I'd like to check these out," with 'these' referring to three books in her arms -- Bend Sinister by Nabakov, Brave New World by Huxley, and Ender's Game by Card. It was an eclectic mix of dystopian novels, though all books I'd read myself in the past. I checked the books out for her, and she went on her way, the two of us flashing smiles to one another at the end of the exchange.

Tori wasn't the prettiest girl I'd ever met by any means. Her form was average as a whole, though her facial structure was a bit chubbier than would be expected for someone her size. She stood five foot, two inches tall, meaning I towered over her by nearly a foot, often leaving me with a wonderful view of both her amber-tinted hair and her pale (though typically cloth-covered) breasts. Tori would return to the library on a weekly basis, usually on Mondays between 2 and 3 in the afternoon, just like clockwork.

Ding-ding. Ding-ding. Ding-ding.

It wasn't until mid-2008 when Tori and I started talking about more than the books she was reading. We ran into each other at the movie theater just up the road from the library. She was going to see "Mirrors" while I had planned to see "Tropic Thunder". I joined her in watching the horror film, though we left within the first hour, choosing instead to spend the remainder of the evening at a park. We dated for sixteen months, typically seeing each other two to three times a week, excluding her weekly library visit. In January of 2010, I proposed to Tori in the Chesterfield County Central Branch library, mere feet from where I had first laid eyes on her. She said yes, and we married in November of that same year.

In May of 2011, Tori developed heavy morning sickness that occurred shortly after she first woke up. Privately, she and I celebrated, assuming that we would soon have an announcement of our first child to give to friends and family. When pregnancy test after pregnancy test came back negative, Tori went to the doctor to see if they could confirm what pee sticks could not. The doctors found that Tori wasn't pregnant, rather that her consistent morning sickness was being caused by a malignant brain tumor. There were concerns early on that the cancer was a metastasis spread from some other region of her body, but doctors found that the cancerous tissue had developed in her brain.

I was devastated by the news. Tori had been my wife for less than a year, and now there was a real chance that I could lose her. If Tori was ever afraid, however, she never showed it to me, even in private. Tori was confident that the doctors would be able to take out all of the tumor with a craniotomy, however tests revealed that there were multiple tumors in her brain, some of which were inoperable.

Ding-ding. Ding-ding. Ding-ding.

Tori tried radiation therapy to rid her brain of the tumors. Early on, Tori found out she'd be losing her long blonde locks, so she dyed them baby blue. Within a few weeks of starting the therapy, her hair loss became so severe that Tori shaved her head, opting instead to wear a short, raven-colored wig. Tori said the black hair made her happy, as going with a blonde color would have made her sad that it wasn't her own hair.

Throughout the entire ordeal, Tori was exceptionally optimistic. While she didn't know if the radiation would cure her cancer, she took solace in her books, adding further value to her weekly trips to the library. Over the last month, as Tori grew weaker and weaker, I took over bringing her books, though her choice of reading has gone from Kafka and Orwell to Seuss and Silverstein, as she found it easier to stay awake for shorter reads.

Three weeks ago, Tori contracted severe pneumonia. The illness, coupled with the weakened state her body was in from radiation, made her extremely frail. I sat by her bedside every night for the past week, barely sleeping as I watched over her. I found myself crying from time to time, afraid of losing her more and more with each passing day. Two nights ago, Tori woke up and caught sight of my tear-covered face. She immediately scolded me for my crying.

"You know that if I die tonight, or whenever, from this horrid disease, it'll be the second best thing that's ever happened to me?" Tori said, her voice faint and calm. "I've been battling for four years through pain and suffering. The physical pain has hurt like hell, but all things considered, it's been tolerable. What's hurt the most is watching how much all of this has hurt you. You're the best thing that's ever happened to me, and I know that you'll miss me if I'm gone. But when I do go, I know that you'll finally have joy in your heart once again because you'll know I'm not hurting anymore."

Ding-ding. Ding-ding. Ding-ding.

Tori fell back asleep after her short speech, her wig sliding off her head as she turned to her side. It would be the last time Tori was awake.

Her body gave out around 7 p.m. last night, with her parents, my parents, and me by her side. I filled out some paperwork at the request of the hospital, grabbed the remainder of Tori's things, and drove back to our small apartment. Within minutes of entering the door, my phone let off its taunting refrain: ding-ding, ding-ding, ding-ding. I knew it was someone telling me that they were sorry for my loss, though I didn't have the heart to see who it was. I placed the phone on Tori's nightstand, where it's laid ever since.

From 10 p.m. on until now (at just past three in the morning), I've sat in our bed, hugging Tori's shirt while watching our wedding DVD on repeat. I haven't shed a single tear, not because Tori wouldn't want me to, but because I know she was right. She doesn't have to feel pain anymore. She can be as happy as I saw her on our wedding day once again. Finally, so can I.

Sadness

At some point in time after Tori's death, someone told me that there were five distinct stages to grieving: denial, anger, bargaining, depression, and acceptance. I can't remember if it was a psychologist, a family member, or someone else altogether who told me this, but apparently all five items are necessary steps to complete in order to move past the grief of losing a loved one. They're a system to finding peace with yourself, with your loss, and with your future.

What people don't realize is that I went through many of these stages myself well before Tori ever died. That's what happens when your wife has a terminal disease. First you can't believe that there's a disease tearing her body apart from the inside, then you're angry (if not livid) that not only is there nothing you can do to help her pain, but that there's nothing you can do to cure her. All you can do is stand back and let the doctors try to save her life. Then comes the bargaining. You don't realize how demeaning begging and pleading with a doctor (or anyone) truly is until you're doing it on a daily basis for nearly six months.

When you realize that your cries to save your wife's life carry little weight beyond a response of "we're doing everything we can for your wife", depression sets in. Tori would have been fully within her rights to tell me to shut up and stop crying at any point during my depression stage. After all, it was her body being ravaged by cancer, not mine. Yet throughout the entire ordeal, I cannot once recall Tori ever saying a bad thing about the disease that was killing her, the way her body was breaking down, or even about how everyone around us changed.

It's amazing watching people in your life vanish like water from a petri dish on a hot summer day. As we all grow older, we grow apart from those to whom we were once close. Childhood and adult friends alike pass by the wayside, and rarely do we give more than a second thought to their disappearance unless we happen to run into them somewhere publicly. Even then, it's rare that you interact with that individual for more than a few minutes, often ending with a forever unfulfilled promise to get drinks or call that person. Even so, it's a typical stage in every person's life. People change, growing apart in the process.

The more maddening fact is when those individuals you've known for forever -- friends as they are initially called -- sink away into the darkness if any sort of trouble befalls you. When I met Tori, she had a wide circle of friends that she hung out with on a fairly regular basis, many of them close girlfriends from her time studying at university. Most were still around well into the first year of our marriage, however when Tori decided to reveal to everyone that she had cancer, those same friends who would drunkenly call her and say they'd stick with her through thick and thin were nowhere to be found. By the end of her first year of treatment, only Johanna, Tori's quiet, church-going ex-roommate, was still around to offer any level of support.

As Tori's health worsened, I found myself withdrawing from my limited social circle as well. You'd think that people would understand that when a terrible illness befalls someone close to you, it means that you may not be as accessible for an extended amount of time. Instead, I rather unexpectedly received complete alienation from my friends. When I did have time away from Tori, I'd try to reach out to my friends, only to have texts and calls go unanswered forever.

That's not to say I lacked people to talk to. The vultures of the medical and legal worlds descended upon Tori and me like crows to carrion on the open

African Savannah. Numerous times per day, we'd both get calls from lawyers, offering us legal help just in case one of the doctors treating Tori were to make a mistake. The lawyers said they were looking out for our best interests, but deep down both they and I knew better. If something did go awry, a medical malpractice suit would have me set for life (not to mention further padding the coffers of that law office and their legal team). But what good is a mountain of money with no use? Sure, the medical bills would be paid off, but I don't need the money for that. If I had money, I'd want to be spending it on having a quality life with Tori, complete with a home that has a white picket fence, a large dog that loves sitting on my lap, and of course the occasional trip to Aruba (as Tori would love). Why would I ask for financial security at the cost of my wife's life?

Last weekend, Tori's gravestone finally went up at Van Delle Cemetery just outside of town. You would be surprised how shiny a gravestone looks when it's first placed. The gleam that radiates from the stone is worn off quickly with the effects of the weather, sun and rain chipping away at its elegance much in the same manner that life slowly chips away at each and every human. For a brief bit of time, however, the headstone will be a bright memorial to my dear wife.

Victoria "Tori" Kirstin Connolly
9/1/1984 - 6/27/2015

Today is my fourth day visiting her grave since the headstone went up. I would have made it a perfect six for six, but my work schedule prevented me from doing much of anything twice this week...one of the items you don't really think about when your wife is receiving cancer treatment is the cost, and I assure you it's been hell to pay for. It's rained all day leading up to my visit, saturating a ground that has already seen more than its fair share of rain this summer. I don't mind visiting the cemetery on rainy days, as they were Tori's favorite times of the year.

I walked up to Tori's grave to find Johanna already sitting on the path at the plot's foot. Her Columbia-colored cardigan had started to turn a darker hue of blue as raindrops continued to pelt her shoulders. Johanna's light ash brown hair was heavy with the weight of water, both from the precipitation and her tears. I placed my hand on her shoulder as I walked up, hoping to calm her sorrow as best as I could. She clutched my wrist with both of her hands, holding on tightly as I stared off towards Tori's headstone.

We stayed in that same position for well over ten minutes, the both of us indifferent to the raindrops beating down on our bodies. Every few minutes, I'd hear Johanna cry out with a soft sob, though she'd try to compose herself through multiple sniffles shortly after. My sadness was more subdued -- after all, Tori had been so upbeat during her entire battle that it was difficult not to share her optimism. Over the past few days though, I felt a growing depression over Tori's death building inside of me. Gone was the one person whose happiness in the face of adversity was so strong that it healed many of my own pains. Behind, all that she left were clothes, pictures, a mountain of medical bills (though this certainly wasn't her fault), and a shiny headstone.

The pain and realization of Tori's permanent demise both hit and overwhelmed me all at once, knocking me from my feet to the wet concrete path below. I curled up on the path and cried, my tears mixing with the puddle of rainwater and mud beneath my face. Johanna hugged my shoulders, quietly whispering that everything would get better with time. As much as I appreciated her effort, I knew better than to believe her. Not every story has a happy ending, especially not for those who deserve it.

I wept for Tori. I wept for myself. I wept for the family we never had. All the while, as I cried, I wondered why I couldn't have Tori back, and if (not when) this dark cloud would clear itself away.

Trust

It's been seven months since Tori died. You'd be surprised how calming of a piece of knowledge it is to know that it's been seven months since she last hurt. I've certainly dealt with grief of my own since then. Yet, as each new day passes, further raising the count of days since Tori's been alive, I get a bit happier, knowing her pain is now gone forever.

Outside of my day-to-day work interactions, I've been fortunate enough to quarantine myself from the world in most instances. The lawyers and doctors have stopped calling, long-lost friends and relatives who claim to be grief-stricken over Tori's death have gone back into the woodwork, and I've stopped getting "I'm sorry" sentiments from every passerby or old lady who checks out a book. Aside from the occasional phone call from my father or my uncle, the only interactions I've experienced have been with Johanna.

Tori and Johanna had roomed together for two years at Rock-Bane College. They were paired together by random chance as enrolling freshman, choosing to live together again during their second year at university. Tori had been going to school to study geology, though she dropped out midway through her third year, moving back home to Chesterland County shortly after. Johanna double majored in psychology and theology, graduating at the top of her class in the process.

Even after they no longer lived together, Tori and Johanna still exchanged phone calls and text messages on a regular basis before Tori passed away. They even went through bouts of writing letters to one another, as if they were third grade pen pals who lived thousands of miles apart rather than a pair of early twenty-somethings who could easily see one another with a 40 minute drive. I'm convinced that Tori would have made Johanna the maid of honor had it not been for Tori's closeness with her sister, Jennifer.

I arrived home at my apartment to find Johanna waiting in the building lobby. Though she had made her way inside, Johanna protected herself from the frigid winter air with a long, burgundy military-style coat, its brass buttons still glimmering from melted snowflakes that had landed upon them.

"Have you been here long?" I asked, stomping the snow off my boots onto the building's entry rug.

"Just a few moments," she replied in a light,

flowing voice. "I tried to time things out to where I wouldn't beat you here, but I guess I didn't plan it out well."

We made our way up the stairs to the top floor of the building and into my apartment. Johanna had been insistent for some time that she wanted to visit me at the apartment; however, I was hesitant to do so. Despite the seven months that had passed since Tori's death, this marked the first time a non-family member had visited me at the home Tori and I used to share (the occasional pizza delivery boy notwithstanding). It was a nerve-wracking occasion and, to Johanna's credit, she could sense that in me. I opened the door and let her in, taking my coat off in the process.

"Do you want me to take your coat?" I offered as I hung my own on a hook beside the main door.

She stood still on my entry mat, not wanting to drip any water from melting snow onto my carpet. "I shouldn't yet. I think you need to hear me out first."

I nodded and made my way back to the kitchen, offering Johanna a drink as I went. I returned with our drinks of choice, a ginger ale for Johanna, and a short glass of honey whisky for myself. Johanna had taken a seat on the far end of my couch, still wearing her coat though she had left her boots at the door. I could see her feet covered in black stockings, indicating she'd likely just come from work as well (she always kept her heels at the office in the winter). Handing her the ginger ale, I made myself comfortable in the armchair to her left, sipping away at my liquor as she began to talk.

"My offer to you is two parts," she began, "though you're not obligated to accept either part or both. I've watched you live without Tori for seven months now. While I lost a friend, you lost more than that. You lost a friend, a wife, a lover, a confidante, and a soulmate. While I wish I could change that loss for you, we both know that there is no amount of power on this Earth that can bring someone back from the dead. All that said, I realize there are many memories around here. Some of these memories are wonderful, harkening back to the happy times you had with Tori. But for most of your marriage, she was in pain, suffering at the hands of a disease that took her life and took your love away.

"Vale, I want to offer you a place to live, first and foremost. I know of a house that's isolated away from town, yet still close enough that your trips to the library wouldn't be more than a short drive by car. It has a second story and a basement, all to go along with a giant barn that you could use to house projects or whatever hobby your heart so desired. Now, you don't have to answer now, but I cert...."

"Yes," I replied, cutting Johanna off.

"But you haven't even heard the rest of the explanation about the house."

"I want away from this place," I said. "You're right, things have been tough these last few months, and I did lose someone who was my entire world. Recently, I've been growing. I've been learning to get past my struggles and grief with Tori being gone. I see this as a wonderful way to help me to further that process."

Johanna appeared surprised by my immediate interest in the house, taking a few moments to collect her thoughts as she sipped her ginger ale. I'd wanted a way to move out of the apartment for some time now. Before Tori was diagnosed with cancer, the two of us had talked about moving out, however I was reluctant to leave my home of six years. When she got sick, we figured the cheap rent was the best option for us financially, and it continued to be for me after her death. Now that I was starting to unbury myself a little from the medical debt, I felt it was time for a new home.

"My second offer may or may not be one you're interested in, but I feel it certainly needs to be pursued."

She stood from the couch and began pacing around the coffee table as she talked. Her coat nearly touched the floor as she walked, though occasionally I'd catch a glimpse of the stockings on one of her legs thanks to a sparkle in the fabric catching my eye.

"When Tori died," Johanna said, "it wasn't because of anything she did."

"I know that," I replied. "She fought the cancer harder than many people do."

"That too, though that wasn't exactly where I was going with this. The night Tori died, I'm willing to bet you that not a single one of those doctors or nurses that worked to try to heal her went home and cried. There was no remorse, no sorrow for one of God's children leaving this world. Even after all their science worked its magic, there was nothing that could be done for her, or so you were told as they wheeled your wife's innocent, though sadly deceased, body off to the mortician's lab. Meanwhile, you're left alone. You've become the latest widow in the scientific war against all that is good and holy. "

I leaned back in my chair, taking an extra-long swig of whisky as Johanna finished her last sentence. I could feel a look of stun creep over my face as I spoke.

"Come again?" I said, perplexed as I'd ever been in my life.

"So...so sorry," Johanna stammered, "let me try explaining this a different way. When Tori went into the hospital for one of her earlier treatments, I went in to visit her. One of the nurses overheard Tori and I talking about how I wanted to help pay for Tori's treatments with money that my church group had raised. Tori, ever the saintly individual, rejected my charity, though the offer led to snickering from two of the nurses walking by the room. That's when I knew the hospital had given up on her. They'd keep her alive long enough to pay for her visits there, but once her useful life had ended, Tori's treatments were bound to be replaced with a placebo of some sort, and she'd die."

It all seemed like an incredible coincidence to me. It was extremely likely that the nurses walking by Tori's room were laughing at a joke they were sharing amongst themselves. Even though a hospital is a rather morbid place, everyone needs humor to get through the day. Tori's condition did begin to take a turn for the worst just as the medical bills were beginning to pile up, though I attribute part of that to my extended absences from work to care for her. And yet, Johanna's confidence in the whole scenario playing out exactly as she stated was unflappable, so much so that as she continued on, I began to believe her.

"Don't let the world fool you, Vale," she continued, "I know you're smart enough to see through their lies. Even if you're not a believer now, I can help you see the light. These medical professionals -- and professional is a term I use extremely loosely in their case -- must pay the price for their sins. The wage of sin is death, and the Devil's already come collecting by taking your dear Tori away. I have lawyer friends who think there's a compelling case to be made here."

"How can I trust that what you're doing is right?" I asked.

"There are some of us in this world who act as mercenaries for what is good and right, even if we have to resort to devious tactics to help find out the truth. I've learned the truth and I want to help you."

"How do I know you're not making all of this up? How can I trust you?"

A small smirk popped up on the right corner of Johanna's mouth. She began to unbutton her coat, holding it tightly together as she did so. As the last button unclasped, she slid the coat to the floor, revealing a cheeky emerald green and black chemise underneath. Her black stockings twinkled with specks of silver and green glitter in them, running up her legs from her feet to the middle of her thighs. Placing one foot in front of the other in a crossing motion, she strode toward my chair, her eyes seductively burning a hole into my soul as she moved.

Johanna stopped at the foot of the chair, wiping her hair away from her left eye as she reached out for my whisky. She consumed the liquor in one gulp, placing the glass on the table beside my chair. Her hands lightly made their way around my chest before pushing me back, reclining the chair in the process. She climbed atop of me, her long legs nuzzling against mine. Her hands gracefully and meticulously made their way into my pants. She clutched her soft hands around my cock as she leaned her face down next to mine, letting her light ash blonde hair dangle on either side of my head as she spoke.

"Let me show you how good trusting someone again can feel."

Disgust

It's a beautiful day to be among the children of our Lord and Savior.

In the month that followed Johanna's seduction of Vale, he found himself to be surprisingly happy. Though the cold winter days dragged on, mirroring his initial apprehension of Johanna's advances, Vale found himself warming up to her as the ambient temperatures rose around him. It was the first time in months that Vale found himself content with life around him, and furthermore the first time in years that he felt secure in how his life was unfolding.

We've become the outcasts of society -- the downtrodden and forgotten of a modern world preoccupied with the desires of man. We are not unlike the Israelites that toiled under the tyranny of the great Egyptian pharaoh long before Moses was sent to take them back to their promised land. God's people were led out of Succoth, out of Pithom, and out of Ra'amses, forward across the Sinai Peninsula and into their promised land, Cannan.

Vale agreed to move into the house that Johanna had offered to help him get, however much to Vale's surprise, Johanna's description of the home as a two-story house with a basement and a barn was an accurate, though incomplete version of reality. The house itself was in terrible disrepair, ravaged by weather and neglect in collaboration with time. While only the kitchen window needed to be replaced, however many of the shutters around the windows -- all once a brilliant baby blue -- were a faded pastel shell of their former selves. A particularly strong storm brought a tree down on the front porch, destroying the front steps and nearly taking out a large bay window that was surely picturesque in its heyday.

God saw that the children of Israel were being oppressed by the Egyptians and he led them out of Egypt. But he didn't do it right away, oh no. Our Lord is a fair and just judge. When God sent Moses, the pharaoh was given an option to free the Israelites from their captivity. In turn, the Lord was affording the pharaoh with an option to save his own detestable nation from certain righteous judgment. Of course, we all know how the story ends. The plagues descended upon Egypt, much of the Egyptian army was swallowed up by the Red Sea, and the people of Israel reached their land, as the Lord had promised.

The second part of the story that Johanna had left out was that she lived at that house. More specifically, she'd turned the loft above the main floor of the barn into a small home, complete with all the rustic conveniences one would expect living atop a countryside barn. Vale's first night in the barn was filled with many sleep-deprived waking moments as nature crept around outside the building's thin wooden walls. The majority of Vale's days off were spent with Johanna trying to turn the broken-down house into a livable location, however even as spring was turning to summer, much of the interior of the home was barely passable for termites, let alone human residency.

While we may be living in the United States rather than Israel, the Book of Exodus has a few lessons we can take away and use in our daily lives. The first is simple -- our Lord will look out for his people. That's been the case since the time of Adam and Eve, and has continued through to modern times. Do you really think the modern state of Israel would exist had God not promised it to David? Man is an inherently selfish being, however even men who don't believe in our Lord can be used as pawns in order for the Lord's will to be fulfilled.

On days where Vale worked at the library, he

found his evenings to be a simple time devoid of house repairs. Typically, Johanna would have a dinner prepared for him by the time he arrived back at the barn, with the meals commonly prepared over an open fire she'd built on the barn's ground floor. The catch of the day was often fish from a stream that ran behind the farm's property, though Johanna would occasionally venture into town to buy chicken or steak if it suited her mood. After a quiet dinner, Johanna would read aloud from her Bible, practicing for her weekly sermon, while Vale worked tree limbs down into walking sticks.

I met a man once. This man had his world crumbling down around him. His wife was dying of cancer. While he still had a job, he was taking off days and weeks at a time to care for his ailing wife. The money they'd saved to send a child they'd never have to college had dried up, and now they were struggling to make ends meet. All the while, doctors and nurses laughed at the man's dying wife. They didn't laugh because of her lack of money nor did they laugh at her cancer -- those are all horrid circumstances that even intellectuals understand. They laughed at her belief in God.

Just after leaving college, Johanna found a job working as a choir director for a local church, thanks in part to her father's friendship with the pastor. When both her father and the church's reverend died in a freak car accident, Johanna convinced the church's leadership to let her lead the church. She stated she found divine inspiration in the words of Christ, though she didn't truly know she was destined to lead her church until she was visited by the spirit of her dead father. The spirit told Johanna it was her mission to bring the world back to the Lord, and to rid it of those who didn't believe in His word, specifically those with high intellectual standing. Despite the shortcomings of the argument, Joanna was put in charge of the church within hours of applying.

For all of their book smarts, all of their degrees, and all of their fancy medicine, those doctors looked down on that man's wife, condemning her to death before she ever had the chance to truly survive. Our God's ways may not always be clear at first. Why would he let these wicked people hurt an innocent woman? I have the answer for you. Sometimes, it's only by the pain of those who are innocent that we are shown the true hatred of the wicked. The sad passing of an innocent woman made her truly strong widow see the world for what it really is.

Johanna's first order of business in leading the church was to encourage her followers to shed any semblance of the intellectual ways of their past. This was handled by having her parishioners bring their books for a mass burning. Of course, it made little sense for Johanna to order the burning of literature, yet to live with a man who worked at a library for a living. She easily passed that off as a way to infiltrate the intellectual agenda. Within weeks of the first book burning, Johanna began delivering her sermons in a slight Southern-U.S. accent that grew more and more pronounced with each passing talk. Her "walk like me, talk like me, be like me, as I'm guided by the Light" mentality caught on quickly throughout the church, and within a few months a small percentage of the quaint Midwestern town's accent-less population sounded like they were lifelong residents of the

Mississippi Delta.

You've all done what the Lord has asked of you through me. You've thrown down the chains of intellectual repression. You've brought your children home to be taught in the way God intended -- by the love of their parents and the wisdom of the land. You've bided your time and you've done very well, dear children of our Lord. Remember though the words of the Book of Matthew, chapter five, verse five. "Blessed are the meek, for they shall inherit the Earth." There has been a promise made to us. Much like God promised the people of Israel the land of Cannan, we have the entire Earth to look forward to.

As the reconstruction of the house transformed the structure from an empty shell into a home, Vale had resorted to turning tree branches into walking sticks and baseball bats. Since Johanna forbade him to read in the barn, it was Vale's most consistent way to release his idle energy on a nightly basis. While he'd made well over forty of the sticks, his favorite was still his first: a thirty-seven inch club made from ash wood that he affectionately referred to as Emma, after the name he and Tori planned to give their first child.

While the Israelites had the plagues that befell Egypt to act as their sign that it was time to rise up and return to Cannan, we must remember that the intellectual world around us has done everything in its power to obscure God's true word from our eyes. We cannot simply wait for a sign. We must rise up now and stop the tyranny and repression that has kept God's people down. While we cannot always fight by the laws of God or the laws of man to win our battles, sometimes it is necessary in the course of preserving justice and all that is holy to act in manners that are neither just nor holy. The war against us has been raging for years. It's time to fight back. And all God's people say...

...amen.

Fear

I awoke in a seated position, my ears tuned to the sounds of a man humming. Neither of those events are incredibly common in my day-to-day life, leading my mind to emotions of confusion and concern. As my field of vision came to, I was startled to find myself roped to a chair, staring at a large cast-iron cauldron filled with water. Pieces of potatoes, carrots, corn, and peas floated atop the water, though it didn't appear as if any source of heat was cooking the food.

Behind me, I could hear the man humming as he chopped away at potatoes, quartering them, and then tossing them over my head as he finished each one. The potatoes made a plopping sound in the water, creating small splashes that landed on the floor beneath my feet. I felt a cold, wet wind whip my right ear as a quartered potato charged by my face, landing in the water with an extra-loud splash. The man chuckled to himself at the sound.

"Good," he said, his voice strung out in a slow, methodical southern drawl. "You've woken up. I thought you would miss dinner."

He laid the knife down, its blade making a clank

against a cutting board, and walked around to my front. He wasn't a particularly tall man, 6'0" or 6'1" at most, with a build resembling that of a long distance runner. He hid a shaved head beneath a light-colored planter's hat, though it was evident from his stubble that he was balding. A light patch of beard hair grew in the form of sideburns on his face, though its color kept it from being visible except in the most direct of light. He smiled as he stood before me, his hands clasped behind his back as he spoke.

"Do you know what it's like to have someone turn down your dinner invitation?" he asked, yet again with a deliberate diction to his words.

"I do not," I replied quietly. Despite the near-whisper level of my speech, my voice echoed throughout the room. A darkness enveloped most of the room, save for the area directly surrounding my person, the man, and the cauldron.

"Of course you don't," he replied. "Ain't much of anyone who knows that feeling anymore, what with social norms and the like. Where are you from, boy?"

"Excuse me?" I asked, indecisive as to if I wanted to answer the man.

He quickly made up my mind for me, grabbing a lengthy wooden rod from beside the cauldron and belting me in the cheek with it. I felt a crack in my jaw as the implement connected, then watched as part of one of my molars flew out of my mouth -- almost as if it were in slow motion -- and collided with the side of the cauldron. The sound of tooth hitting iron resonated throughout my mind. He picked up the shard of bloody tooth off the ground, chuckling all the while. He placed the tooth in his pocket and responded to my question.

"You have two strikes left, you know. I'm not a man who wants or needs all that much. I have a home, I have my girl, and I have my whisky. All I need that I can't get on my own is food, company, and coitus. I promise I didn't bring you here to fuck you, so I'll leave you with the choice as to which of the others you want to be. Now...let's try this again. Where are you from, boy?"

My jaw stung as I spoke my response to the man. "I'm from Lansing, Michigan, sir."

"Sir!" the man responded. "Well now I guess they do still teach manners in heathen states. Do you remember me?"

I looked him over for nearly a minute, trying to place where I'd seen the man before. His face did look slightly familiar, though not for any reason I could recall. His question led me to believe I should know who he is, and I even considered making up a memory of him for a brief second. I thought better of it, figuring he'd be more offended by a lie than by my lack of memory.

"No, sir, I don't believe I do."

"Seems about right. I didn't reckon that you would. You see, two days ago, you drove through my town, stopping to fuel your car at the lone gas station in town. Your car was covered in streamers and window paint declaring how its occupants were 'just married'. I chuckled to myself as I watched you get out of your car and pump gas in a tuxedo you'll never wear again. I sat on my rocking chair in front of the library, laughing a bit too much at your attempts to fuel your car while your wife was in the convenience store.

"I shouted at you," he continued, "inviting you and your bride to come have dinner with me. You'd be my guests of honor, man and soon to be freshly fucked wife, at a dinner fit for a king, or at least all that I could afford. When you didn't respond, I figured there's a chance you were hard of hearing like my father, so I shouted again louder. And what did you do, boy?"

"I finished filling up then got in the car," I answered.

"And why did you do that?"

I took a deep breath, afraid as to how he might respond to my honest answer. That said, honesty had gotten me by once before, so I might as well try it again.

"I thought you were a drunk rambling on about nothing important."

Shot number two from the stick landed across the right side of my face just to the right of my eye. The pain with this hit was far more severe, and despite my best efforts, I could neither see from nor stop the watering from my right eye. Through my remaining good eye, I watched the man tap the stick on the ground at my feet, his face retaining its stoic smile.

"That's two strikes," he said. "You know what they say happens when you have three strikes, so I wouldn't say the wrong thing again."

He walked behind me, pouring some sort of liquid into a pair of glasses. I heard him take a long drink as he strode toward me, his breath devoid of alcohol in spite of the overpowering scent coming from somewhere. As he pushed a glass to my lips, I found the source of the smell, as the taste of moonshine burned away at my aching, bleeding mouth.

"I didn't figure you'd like real milk, so this was the next best thing I had. All you city boys are so stuck on your pasteurization and your soy-based drinks that you wouldn't know natural if it walked up and kicked you in your testicles. Tell me about your wife. What's her name?"

Despite my pain, I lashed out in anger at the man. "What the fuck do you mean 'what's her name'? You tell me your fucking name."

"Now, now," he replied, "There's no need to get angry. Perhaps I should have introduced myself before Emma here hit you across the face twice. Frankly, my name isn't that important in the grand scheme of things. I've been called a coward and a drunk, a liar and a sinner, a deviant and a madman. That said, I've also been called a saint and a good man, a lover and a friend, a husband and a widow. I'm a free-thinker and a free mind, I'm the consciousness of your mind and the blood inside your heart, I am everything that you wished you could be all while being everything that you strive never to become.

"Name? I don't need a name. But since it's polite to provide you with one as a guest, my name is Vale Connolly. Now, if you please, share your name and your wife's name with me so that we don't have to talk in vague answers."

Content that Vale had opened himself up to me a little, I responded to his question, hoping to humanize my wife -- wherever she was – and me to this man.

"My name is Adam Grigson, and my wife is Brianna Grigson. I'm from Lansing, Michigan while she's from Battle Creek. We've been married three days now, at least based off of when you saw us at the gas station, and we were en route to our honeymoon in Portland, Oregon."

Vale turned around and plucked half of a carrot from the caldron behind him, chomping on it quietly as he spoke on.

"Brianna," he began, "That's a pretty name for a pretty lady. Now before you go worrying about her, she's perfectly safe inside my house. She's got nothing at all to worry about."

"Why do you have us here?" I asked.

"And now you begin asking the right questions," Vale responded. "These are the questions you should have been asking all along. As I sat on my rocking chair at the library laughing at your misfortune, I frankly thought nothing more of you than I would the bowel movement I take each morning. But then...then I saw your wife. You see, she's Brianna to you, but to me, she's a vision of something long-lost. I was once just married, the same as you are now. My wife was a beautiful short blonde woman named Tori, whom your Brianna bears a striking resemblance to.

"Tori and I were married for five years, four of which was spent living with her dying of a cancer that doctors couldn't stop. For four years, they tried everything they could to keep her alive, yet they failed. The funny thing is, it wasn't even the cancer that took her from me. It was pneumonia. Her body was so weak thanks to the radiation the doctors used to fight the cancer that she couldn't fight off a simple cold, leading it to turn into something far worse.

"What's your favorite vegetable, Adam?"

"I...I like tomatoes," I answered, completely perplexed by his question. "Why?"

Vale sighed and shook his head at me, eying the stick -- its name apparently Emma -- that rested to his left.

"I'm tempted to correct you physically for that misstep; however I'm willing to place the blame for your ignorance on the American education system and not on you. It's acceptable that you don't know such a fact. The doctors who worked on Tori, however...for them it wasn't acceptable. In my mind, when you're smart enough to be a doctor, you should be smart enough to know that a tomato is, in fact, a fruit, and not a vegetable. I may talk slow, but I'm not stupid. I know that a tomato is a fruit.

"Have you been wondering why the lights are low in here? Have you wondered why the only things you can see in this room are you, this cauldron, Emma, and I? It's fairly simple really. If I turned on the lights, I'd have to kill you for what you saw, and I've yet to decide if that's necessary. I can tell you that there are pictures of my wonderful Tori all over the walls of this room. Along with those pictures hang the skeletons of every single doctor and nurse that worked on Tori and couldn't save her life. Every. Last. One."

Vale picked up Emma and began circling my chair, tapping the wooden rod against my ankles as he made his rounds. On his fourth trip around me, Vale stopped and straddled my lap, sitting down on my now-asleep legs. Through my one good eye, I could see his cold brown eyes, devoid of any feeling or misery for what he'd done to the doctors whose bones hung around me. He gave me a stern look, his mouth moving just inches from mine as he spoke.

"Realistically, Adam, you have three options," said Vale. "Your first option is to try to run, but you won't get very far tied to that chair. If you do try to run, Emma here will put a lengthy, violent, bloody end to you. Your second option is to stick around and join your wife, my housemate, and I for dinner. Now, unlike the first option, you'll be eating dinner with us instead of being dinner, however there's no guarantee I'll keep you around long after seeing you and your wife back together. Jealousy is a hateful bitch. Your third option is to let me knock you out and take you somewhere safe. You'll never know where I am, you won't see your wife again, but you'll get to live."

"How do I know you're going to keep your word about my safety?" I asked.

Vale rose from my legs, twirling Emma around in the air as he laughed. As the stick came down into his hands again, he laughed and took a mighty swing.

"Strike three. Good night."

Anger

"Wake up, my dear. It's time to eat."

Brianna swam through a groggy haze, trying to will herself out of her slumber. Sounds of a man and a woman talking outside of her room filled Brianna's throbbing head, the voices bouncing around in a cacophony of words. Slowly, she worked her eyes open, finding herself in a small room lined with unpainted drywall. She was lying in a bed covered by a crimson comforter and pale pink sheets. At the foot of the bed stood a small brown dresser, its wood worn and weathered, though it appeared structurally sound. Atop that dresser sat a glass of water and a pile of clothes, both neatly placed far away from the dresser's edge.

Brianna climbed out of bed and made her way to the dresser, finding herself completely nude as she did so. On top of the clothes sat a small yellow envelope with the words "For You" scrawled across the front in a barely legible handwriting. Brianna opened the envelope, producing a greeting card covered in roses that surrounded the words "Welcome Home." As Brianna opened the card, a photograph fell to the floor, landing face down at her feet. Leaving the picture at her feet, Brianna read the carefully written message inside the card.

It's been far too long since I last saw you
I hope you like the clothes I picked out for you...
...we can always get you new ones if you don't.
It's the first day of your new life, Tori.
Welcome home.

The card was unsigned, leaving Brianna no clues as to who it was from. Last she remembered, she was laying down to sleep in a hotel room with her new husband, Adam, as they made their way on a cross-country honeymoon road trip. Now, unpainted walls and unfamiliar clothing that she reluctantly put on her body to cover herself up were the only things Brianna knew about her location. Most of the clothes fit her perfectly, though the yellow blouse was about a half-size too big. She felt uncomfortable in these unfamiliar clothes and surroundings.

She picked up the photograph that had landed at her feet, staring at it contemplatively. Brianna found the woman in the picture to be strikingly similar to her in appearance, though it was evident to Brianna that there were difference in the curvatures of their respective jawlines, not to mention a strong difference in the shade of blonde hair that each had. Flipping the picture over, Brianna found a fading sentence written on the back of the picture in a delicate, feminine handwriting.

Happy anniversary. I love you. -T

Brianna placed the picture on the dresser and left the bedroom. She made her way down a dim, unpainted hallway, working her way toward the voices she heard earlier. As she neared the light of the next room, the voices became clearer, with a man and a woman yelling at each other in somewhat hushed tones.

"For fuck sake, Vale, I don't get why you're pussying out on this now," said the woman. "We've made such great progress for you, for the church, and for the world."

"Johanna, it's not that simple," replied Vale, "I couldn't just kill him."

"Why not?" Johanna retorted. "You didn't have any trouble killing those doctors and nurses."

"We're taking away a man's wife. You don't know what that feels like. I couldn't take away his wife and kill him. It hurt me with every shot I took at him to knock him out."

Brianna froze in place and listened quietly while Vale and Johanna argued. She felt fortunate that neither of them had heard her make her way into the hallway, though Brianna knew it was only a matter of time before one of them (if not both) came looking for her.

"All you've done is interrupted God's Will, Vale," Johanna said, her voice raising louder and louder as she continued to speak. "What did you do with him?"

Vale cleared his throat, trying to calm himself before he answered. "I knocked him out and dumped him about ten miles out of town. He'll never know where he was and he doesn't know enough to find his way back here to try to get his wife back."

The sound of a slap echoed throughout the building, reverberating in Brianna's ears before combining its echoes with the sounds of Johanna's shrill retort.

"Would you stop calling her his wife?" Johanna yelled. "After all of the fighting we've done, you honestly believe I'd have you save the life of some random schmuck's wife? Are you fucking dense? That IS Tori. God has allowed her to have new life on this Earth and has destined her to be here with me again."

"No, her name is Bria..."

Vale stopped midway through his statement as if a light switch flipped in his brain. He strode to a kitchen chair, scooting it away from the table. Vale sat down to collect his thoughts.

Johanna grew impatient with Vale's lack of words, choosing to go back to carving the beef roast she'd prepared for dinner. Brianna peeked around the corner and watched as Vale stared silently into space, his eyes flickering and buzzing with deep, purposeful thoughts. It was if a metamorphosis was occurring in his brain, changing from cocoon to butterfly as his thoughts became more intense. Though Brianna couldn't imagine his thoughts, something told her that Vale had found a renewed purpose in his verbal spat with Johanna. Vale rose from his chair, leaning against the table as Johanna continued to cut the roast.

"What do you mean here with you again?" Vale asked, a vicious glare covering his face. "She was my wife. What happened between you and Tori that you haven't been telling me?"

"Despite the fact that I allow you to speak eloquently at home, you're a rather simple man, Vale," responded Johanna as she pulled the meat fork and knife from the roast, letting the last piece of meat fall haphazardly onto its serving tray. "It's too bad this isn't a simple answer. Tell me...what would you do to be with Tori again?"

"You know damn well I'd do anything to be with Tori."

"Glad to see that hasn't changed. Let me help you out with your desires."

With a quick movement of her left hand, Johanna slashed the carving knife across Vale's neck and collarbone. As he reached to clutch the open wound, Johanna stabbed the meat fork into his hand, placing the tines around his ring and index fingers, surrounding his middle metacarpal in the process. Johanna deftly moved toward Vale's stunned body, tackling him into the wall and rattling pictures in the hallway. One of the pictures fell at Brianna's feet, glass shattering on the ground and surrounding her.

Johanna began to wail away on Vale, delivering

a series of punches and elbows to the open wound on Vale's neck. With each strike, Vale choked more and more, a stringy mix of spit and blood rolling out of his mouth and drooling onto his shoulder. As Vale's eyes began to droop toward closing, Johanna climbed off his body and made her way toward the kitchen cabinets. From a door above the sink, she produced a .22 caliber handgun, an empty magazine, and a small package of bullets. As Johanna loaded the magazine, she spoke to Vale in a stern tone reminiscent of one of her sermons.

"There was no sense of 'anything' that happened between Tori and I," Johanna began, "but that doesn't mean there shouldn't have been. She was my best friend. We were destined to be together in some sense, be that living together, sharing our lives together as partners, or even just as the best friends we were. But she got taken away -- not by God nor by cancer -- she got taken away by these so-called brilliant minds of the world who do nothing but conspire to weed out the righteous and the meek. Unfortunately for Tori, her cancer made her meek, and her love for the Lord made her righteous. That's what killed her.

"Exacting revenge on Tori's doctors and nurses was never going to bring Tori back to life, neither for you nor for me. I've known that for a long time. It was merely a catalyst for the pious of the world to rise up against the tyranny of intellectualism and overthrow our captors. I knew full well going into this that there was a good chance that you and I both would die as martyrs for the greater good of the world. That said, it seems that all you want to die for is the memory of Tori, while I've found a suitable replica of her embodiment here on Earth."

Johanna snapped the now-filled magazine of ammunition into the gun, making her way to Vale's feet. His eyes had completely closed, his life slowly fading away as blood poured from his body onto the floor. Johanna placed the gun in the middle of Vale's forehead and spoke to him yet again.

"On the third day, our Lord rose again from the grave, yet you doubt his capability to bring a woman back to life? We must cast out the doubters, for they are like a plague to our church, and so out is where you will go. Yea, though I walk through the valley of the shadow of death, I will fear no evil, for the Lord is with me. His rod and his staff, they comfort me. They will lead me forth to carry out the Lord's commands, lest the world's wishes become a burden unto my feet. And it is for this reason that I -- unlike you -- will dwell in the house of the Lord, forever."

Johanna quickly fired off a trio of shots into Vale's head, then pushed his body down to the floor. She unloaded the magazine from the gun, meticulously removing the remaining bullets from the clip and placing them back into their packaging. She then made her way to the hallway to find Brianna curled up on the floor in tears, visibly shaken from the sounds of death emanating from the next room. Johanna knelt down in the broken glass and cradled Brianna's body, holding her in an attempt to comfort her.

"Shhh...it's all going to be alright," Johanna said as she ran her bloody fingers through Brianna's hair. "It's all going to be okay. You're home now, Tori. No one is ever going to take you away from me again."

Surprise

What had been a loud and alarming morning transitioned into a surprisingly quiet afternoon for Brianna. Glass from the picture frame in the hallway had cut her foot, albeit not badly. Despite the wounds not being serious, Johanna took a significant amount of time to be sure they were bandaged up properly, even giving Brianna a pair of shoes to protect her just in case any residual shards remained in the hall.

Johanna encouraged Brianna to take a nap in order to relax after the stress of the morning. Brianna obliged, waking up to a completely clean hallway and kitchen. Johanna was in the process of scrubbing the final splatter marks of Vale's blood off the wall when Brianna sleepily walked around the corner.

"Well hello there," Johanna said, her face beaming with a wide smile, "I'm so happy to see that you're awake, Tori."

Brianna stared blankly at Johanna's eager face, perplexed at her excitement. While she had overheard much of Vale and Johanna's argument about her, Brianna figured that when Johanna called her Tori, she meant it metaphorically. Still, Brianna decided it would be in her best interest to be cautious about how she went about trying to correct Johanna, particularly considering she had just killed a man in cold blood over his disagreement on the same point.

"I'm sorry," began Brianna, "but I don't know who you are."

"Oh, dear, I should have known better. Death does strange things to people. I shouldn't expect you to remember everything right away. Come with me."

Johanna grabbed Brianna's hand and led her into the house's spacious living room. A large, black leather couch sat against the room's far wall, flanked by a pair of gigantic mahogany bookshelves. Johanna led Brianna to the couch, then contemplatively stared at the bookshelf nearest to her. After a few moments of pondering, she grabbed a small, yellow photo album before sitting down on the couch next to Brianna. Johanna placed the spine of the photo album in the small gap between their legs, opening it up so that the left side of the album sat on her legs, while the right side rest on Brianna's.

"Your name is Tori Connolly," Johanna said, doing her best to stare into Brianna's eyes as she spoke, "though when you and I met, your name was Tori Landon. And my name is Johanna DeMay. You grew up not too far from here in rural Chesterland County as the second child of six. You were part of a very close family that loved you very much, though during your last couple of years on this Earth -- well, at least the ones before now -- you didn't talk to them very much because you were sick."

"I was sick?" Brianna asked, attempting to humor Johanna. Brianna had already begun forming a plan to run away in the middle of the night while Johanna slept, however she needed to make it through the rest of the day before that could come to fruition.

"You died of cancer in the summer of 2015, just under two years ago. It was a very sad and trying time for all of us."

"Who is all of us?"

"That's a bit of a tricky question," responded Johanna. "Obviously, it was a rough time for your family, even though you talked with them a bit less. I spent a good amount of time with you at the hospital, though I admit I wasn't around as much as I would have liked to have been for you, thanks to my obligations with the church. Your husband was pretty broken up by your death too, though I honestly don't think he was as upset about your passing as I was."

"Was that man you killed earlier my husband?" Brianna asked.

Johanna sighed and bowed her head to her chest, muttering a barely audible prayer to the heavens. Brianna heard the word 'patience' slip from her lips more than once, though the rest of the plea was largely garbled. Johanna finished her prayer, then looked up at Brianna. Johanna's face filled with the same excited smile Brianna saw in the kitchen a few minutes prior.

"Yes, that man was your husband, Tori," Johanna replied. "His name was Vale Connolly, and the two of you had been married for about five years when you died. The two of you met at the library in town -- the same one I would drop you off every Monday during your last semester at school -- though you didn't really talk about him all that much until you moved out from our apartment."

"So I lived with you at one point?"

"Quite a while actually. We lived together for nearly three years while we were both at college. You may have married Vale, but your first love was God. After nineteen years of having a love only for the Lord, I was your second love. This picture here was from the start of our second year in college. Just look at the way you and I have our arms around each other. While that may have been the early stages of attraction, it's evident that there was chemistry between you and me."

Brianna stared at the picture for a moment. In the photo, seven girls posed together with their arms around one another and bright smiles on their faces. Johanna was on the far left end of the group, both of her arms tightly wrapped around the neck of the girl beside her, presumably Tori. While Johanna wore a beaming smile, it was evident that Tori realized how close Johanna was to her right as the picture was taken, as her face had shifted into a look of equal parts smile and horror. Johanna turned the page and began talking about another picture.

"This one is from your 21st birthday," Johanna said. "You had a few too many drinks and tried to go home with some sleezeball guy from Delta Chi, though I wasn't about to let that happen. We both stumbled back to the apartment where you puked out your guts for a good half hour while I held your hair back. We got you all cleaned up and ready for bed, after which you thanked me by kissing me for the first time. We fell asleep together -- sleep sleep, not sleeping together like sex -- though when the morning came you apologized for how awkward it was that we both slept in my bed."

Johanna sat the photo album on Brianna's lap and walked to the entryway of the house. From the entry closet, she produced a tattered purple blouse with white stitching. Johanna walked back to the couch, handing the shirt to Brianna while taking the album in her own hand. Johanna flipped the page of the album to show a picture of Johanna with Tori, who was wearing the same purple top that Brianna now held.

"That blouse you're holding was one of my gifts to you for your 22nd birthday," continued Johanna.

"You told me it was such a surprise that I got you a present, especially considering that for the four birthdays prior, we'd just found a way to buy each other alcohol. I wanted to give you something you could use, but to be honest, I wanted to give you myself. The problem was you'd found yourself a boyfriend...not Vale, it was some other guy who didn't last all that long...so my alternate offer wasn't exactly an option. I always figured you'd find your way back to me, especially after that kiss. Though Vale delayed that for quite a while, I think we've been given a second chance."

Johanna rose from the couch and put the photo album back in the bookshelf. As she looked through the other albums on the shelf, sirens began to go off in Brianna's head about Johanna's relationship with Tori. The term star-crossed lovers was an expression Brianna had heard before in movies to describe lovers who are perfect together but were never meant to be with one another. It was quickly becoming evident that Johanna viewed herself and Tori as star-crossed lovers who were never able to be together in life, but a rebirth of that lover (albeit by proxy) was the solution for love to exist.

As Johanna made her way to the couch with an arm full of photo albums in hand, Brianna noticed that the sirens going off in her head were not just figments of her imagination, but the sounds of actual sirens getting progressively louder. As the wail of the sirens reached ear-piercing levels, they abruptly began to wind down. A quick glance to the doorway revealed flashes of red and blue lights outside the house. Johanna was the first to notice the lights, setting the books down and making her way to the kitchen as the lights grew brighter. Brianna timidly curled up in the corner of the couch, doing everything in her power to calm herself as a man's voice boomed over a megaphone.

"Vale Connolly and Johanna DeMay. We have a warrant for your arrest for the abduction of Adam and Brianna Grigson, as well as on suspicion of various other crimes. Come out of the house with your hands in the air."

Anticipation

As police lights flashed outside of the house, Brianna stared intently at Johanna's purposeful movements in the kitchen. She watched as Johanna ducked around the room's window, gliding from cabinet to cabinet as she produced weapon after weapon from the room's storage. Johanna's movements were swift and fluid, almost as if she'd been preparing for such an occurrence well in advance of the police arriving today. The megaphone from outside broke through the sounds of Johanna's movements, its blaring vocal tones echoing throughout the house.

"Vale and Johanna, we know you're in there," the man speaking into the megaphone said. "We want a peaceful solution to this situation. Come out with your hands up and we can talk this through."

Johanna strode back into the living room, a pair of rifles under one arm while the gun she used to kill Vale was in her other hand. She set the weapons down on the couch beside Brianna, speaking as she made her way to the kitchen a second time.

"What they don't realize is that we've both been far worse places than staring down the barrel of a gun," Johanna said as she picked up yet another hunting rifle. "They think that death can scare us, but they don't realize that we're not afraid to die."

"Honestly," Brianna stammered, "I--I'm actually quite afraid of dying. If you could do something so that I don't die, that would be lovely."

Johanna laid two more rifles down next to Brianna, placing a serving bowl full of ammunition nearby. She knelt at Brianna's feet, pulling her body close for a tight embrace. Brianna squirmed cautiously in an attempt to free herself from the hug, but with every movement found herself even closer to Johanna's body.

"I know you don't want to die, Tori," Johanna stated as she ran her fingers through Brianna's hair, "and I promise you I'm going to do everything in my power to be sure that nothing happens to either one of us. I just need you to remember that our Lord has a place for us in Heaven where we'll never hurt again. If something happens to us here today, I know that I'll see you there, just as my faith has brought you back alive for me now."

Johanna walked toward the entryway, where the front window was open ever so slightly. Her approach to the window was partially obscured by the purple curtains that hung from the rod above the window, but it was evident to those outside that someone was coming closer. As Johanna reached the window, Brianna slid the .22 handgun onto her lap, clutching its stock tightly as Johanna yelled out the window.

"Officers," Johanna shouted, "I understand that you're only doing your job, and I commend you for that. There needs to be more people willing to stand up for what's right in the world, and rest assured I do appreciate your efforts. However, you're interfering with our Lord's divine destiny, and for that there is no one to answer to but our God himself."

"Johanna, we don't want any trouble," the megaphone yelled back. "We have a warrant for the arrest of you and Vale Connolly. We can do this peacefully, we just need you to come out of the house."

"You don't understand what you're doing,

officers," responded Johanna. "Vale died earlier today. There's no one here but me and my darling, Tori. And that is a reality that came to be only through divine providence -- an intervention by the most holy being in the world Himself. If you're looking to make amends with any wrong Vale committed in this world, I'd be happy to help you tie up any loose ends. But with that though, realize that God's purpose is not for me to go with you."

"Johanna DeMay, you have three minutes to exit the house with your hands in the air. If you don't, we will be forced to come in after you."

As Johanna turned from the window to make her way back to the living room, Brianna covered the handgun on her lap with the purple blouse that Johanna had handed her just minutes prior. As she neared the couch, Johanna stopped at the bookshelf, producing a sealed green envelope from between two copies of the Bible. She sat cross-legged on the floor at Brianna's feet, placing a rifle beside her as she opened the envelope.

"For seven months after you died," Johanna began, "I came to your grave twice a week. I prayed to God that he'd give me my Tori back from those who had taken you away from me. Some days I wanted to go, but I could not bring myself to do so. The reason I couldn't go wasn't because I missed you -- that's the biggest reason I kept coming. There were times my faith was tested. These were times where I wasn't sure that the Lord was going to answer my prayers. I wrote you a letter one of those nights, just in case I ever got to see you again. Would you mind if I read it to you, Tori?"

Brianna nodded as her hands fumbled with the handgun on her lap. The purple blouse had started to slide off the gun's grip, however Johanna was so engrossed by opening the letter that she didn't notice Brianna adjust the shirt, covering the weapon up again.

"It's dated October 31, 2015," Johanna began. "My dear Tori. It's been over four months since I last saw you alive. There isn't a day that goes by where you're absent from my thoughts. I thought I knew what pain was. I lost my oldest sister at age seven, my younger sister at age 14, mother at 17, and my father at 25. All that was left in my life was my religion and my best friend -- you. Even though you've been married for some time, meaning that I didn't get to talk to you as much as we used to, I know that you were always there for me.

"It took me time to come to grips with the fact that you didn't see me in the same light as I saw you. To you, I was the annoying, though not intolerable roommate who didn't want to hang around with anyone but you. I shared too much information on a regular basis, I tried to become way too involved in your personal life, and I wanted to be everywhere you were. Eventually, that desire for friendship became something more. You were the first person of any gender I was ever attracted to, and while I realize that many facets of my religion frown upon homosexuality, I also realize that our Lord wants us to love each other equally. He's always going to protect me even if my love answers to She instead of He.

"I know you never liked me that way, at least nothing beyond a curiosity on a very drunken night.

That was very hard for me to accept, and to be honest, it took you laying in a hospital bed with a terminal disease to realize I was willing to accept you just being my friend. It was at that point when I also saw that you truly loved me for the first time. Sure, it was not the same type of love I had for you once upon a time, but it was the love of a friend. It was a love that realized I was going to be there by your side in life as well as in death.

"I've been praying to God that he gives me another way to be with you on Earth, even if it is just for one more day. As much as I believe in His will, there are times I don't know if He'll make this happen. But I have faith that you're watching over me too, and that you'll help me find a way for this to happen. And even if I never see you again on Earth, I know you'll be the first one to embrace me when I join you in Heaven. I love you. Johanna."

Just as Johanna finished reading the letter, the police burst through the door. The monstrous sound of the front door being kicked open cut through Brianna's eardrums, intensifying the flow of tears that streamed down her face from hearing Johanna's letter. A tall man in combat gear pointed an assault rifle at Johanna and began shouting.

"Johanna DeMay, you're under arrest," he yelled. "Lay on the ground and put your hands behind your back."

Johanna calmly set the letter down in front of her and looked up to face Brianna. A peaceful, serene look had come over Johanna's face, filling her words with calmness and sincerity as she spoke.

"I'm really sorry I got you involved with this, Brianna," Johanna said. "Thank you for being my link to what I once had."

Johanna quickly turned and reached for the rifle at her side. The policeman shot instinctively as she did so, a pair of bullets sinking into Johanna's back and through her lungs. With one last lunge, Johanna tried to turn and fire, only to be hit with three more projectiles. The rifle fell to the ground by Johanna's side as her head collapsed onto the letter she'd written for Tori.

The policeman stared at Johanna's body for a few moments, making sure that she was no longer of any danger to anyone in the room. Once he was certain, he turned to Brianna and reached out his hand.

"Brianna Grigson?" he asked.

"Yes I am." she replied.

"Let's get you back somewhere safe. I'm sorry you had to see that."

Brianna started to move her legs to stand, but thought better of it as she remembered the gun in her lap. She looked up at the officer, her tear-stained face illuminated by the setting sun coming from the window behind her.

"Is my husband alive?" she asked.

"I'm afraid not," the policeman replied, "he died in the hospital this afternoon shortly after we talked to him."

Brianna rose to her feet, revealing the weapon in her hand as the blouse that was covering it hit the floor. The policeman sprang back to attention immediately upon seeing the gun, though quickly realized the weapon wasn't meant for him.

"Brianna," he said, "I realize you've been through a lot this week. You've gone through more pain in these few days than I'd wish on anyone. Please, put the gun down. We'll get you to a hospital, we'll make sure you're all right, and we'll get you through all of this."

Brianna continued raising the gun to her temple, the cold metal of the barrel pressing against her throbbing blood vessels as she did so. Though tears continued to flow freely from her eyes, Brianna reflected the same calm facial expression that Johanna had shown to her just moments prior.

"Dying for someone you love isn't a death sentence at all. If anything, it's how we give birth to new life. To ask for divine providence otherwise is to truly die."

As Brianna readied herself to pull the trigger, all she could hear was the sound of the blood in her body rushing through the vessels in her head.

Thump-thump. Thump-thump. Thump-thump.

Amid the repetitive drumming of her heartbeat in her head, Brianna heard a shot ring out, combining its melodic explosion with the tones of her pulse into the sound of bells in her ears.

Ding-ding. Ding-ding. Ding-ding.

She collapsed to the floor beside Johanna, the repetitive ringing still sounding through her ears. In death, Johanna looked happy, finally reunited with the woman -- the friend -- she so dearly missed. Brianna felt herself lifted off the ground and being carried away into the distance, Johanna's smile getting more and more faint with each passing moment. Brianna felt weightless, as if all of her senses were free...all but one.

Ding-ding. Ding-ding. Ding-ding.

AWKWARD?

Tony and Melissa's first date was like many other first dates that would take place that particular Friday evening in Glendale. They would meet at a small, yet heavily visited coffee shop, sharing coffee before they decided if they liked each other enough to go to a movie. Melissa's commute to the date would be short, as she lived in Glendale, while Tony drove across the valley from his home in Chandler to the date.

The two arrived within minutes of each other, Tony just before the agreed upon time of 7:00 p.m., with Melissa arriving at 7:03 p.m. Tony wore his nicest -- and only -- dress shirt, a pale blue polo that was a touch too tight around his stomach, yet too loose on his neck. His pants were a faded pair of blue jeans that he had bought at a local thrift store days prior, finding them both functional and affordable at one dollar for a pair of pants with three working pockets. Melissa's blouse sported a floral pattern not unlike those found on a 1970's casting couch. Earlier in the day, Melissa had made the conscious decision to wear light grey leggings with the top instead of pants, a decision that she both regretted and reveled in upon seeing Tony's bargain bin chic.

As Melissa and Tony strode toward each other in the busy establishment, the sexual tension escalated with every movement they made. With each step, Tony stared deeply into Melissa's eyes, while Melissa's left eye returned the favor. Her right eye stared lackadaisically off to the side, eye fucking an empty table and chairs as she passed. Tony reached out and extended his hand to meet Melissa's.

"Hi, I'm Tony," he stated. "Or Anthony. Or Anth. Really you can call me whatever you want."

"You look like a young Gilbert Gottfried," Melissa said, fawning over Tony's curly hair as she shook his sweaty hand.

"Thanks. I washed my armpits today."

Tony and Melissa strode toward the barista at the counter. The barista twirled his handlebar mustache as he asked for their order.

"Oh, order me something that I'll like, Tony," said Melissa as she tugged on his arm.

"Well, I'm not sure what you like," Tony replied, "but I can try. Barkeep, give me a small white chocolate mocha and..."

"Tony, I'm allergic to chocolate."

"Sorry. How about a small chai tea?"

"Can't have it. Tea makes me gassy on weekdays."

"Italian soda?"

"My grandpa died eating a stromboli. Italian soda brings back bad memories."

The barista walked away from the counter as Tony and Melissa bantered back and forth about what drinks to order. He grabbed a pair of cans of diet cola, slowly pouring the liquid into tall glasses, so as not to overflow the containers with foam. He carried both glasses to the counter, placing them before Tony and Melissa.

"It sounds like what you two need is a glass of something with fake sugar in it," the barista said. "It's on the house, and so's the obesity it'll cause."

"Thank you so much!" Melissa said excitedly. "I love diet drinks!"

The regular evening crowd had already filled most of the tables at the coffee shop. Nevertheless, Tony and Melissa were able to find a quiet, secluded table next to the restrooms to share. Melissa sat in her chair and began sipping her drink, while Tony dug through his pockets, producing a handful of strawberry candy. He placed it on the table between the two of them as he began to speak.

"Tell me about yourself, Melissa," he said.

"Well, I'm the third child of four," Melissa began. "I have two older sisters, Kerri and Mia, and a younger brother, Dan. Dan is a fan of masturbating outside the bathroom while I shower. He's still a young kid, so I'm sure he'll grow out of it."

"How old is Dan?"

"Twenty-six. Tell me about you."

"For starters, I've been arrested twice for stalking my ex-girlfriend," said Tony. "I really feel like the restraining order is helping me get over her, though I'll still log in to her email and read messages from her husband to see if I get angry. It happens less often, so I think I am making progress. Oh, and I have a pet leopard that I keep in my basement."

"That's so adorable!" Melissa exclaimed, her eyes wide with excitement. "I love animals! What's his name?"

"Deaf. Where do you see this date going?"

"That honestly depends. I'd love to go see a movie and give you a blowjob in the back of the theater; however I have to work later tonight, so I don't know how long I could stay."

Tony checked his phone to see the time. It was 7:17 already, making this his longest date in three years. Each passing second gave him more confidence, so he pressed on, placing his hand over Melissa's as he spoke.

"Where do you work at that you have to go to work so late?" Tony asked.

"I'm a janitor at a strip club," replied Melissa. "It's not good money most nights, but occasionally one of the dancers will drop a $20 out of her g-string on the way to the back and I'll find it. I think of it as my tip for my trouble. What about you?"

"I'm in between jobs now. Well, more like in between jobs...and houses."

"You poor thing! Where do you sleep at night? What about Deaf?"

"I lied," Tony replied, "I don't have a leopard anymore. Or a basement. Or a place to live. I usually sleep in my car, though there are some nights I can find my way into a hotel if I do a few odd jobs for the desk clerk. I gave the leopard to a one-armed drummer I met behind a meth lab."

Melissa sprang up from her chair, tossing her purse around her shoulder as she stood. She grabbed Tony's hand and led him toward the door.

"Where are we going?" Tony asked.

"To make babies."

USE AS DIRECTED

I was told to write in stream of consciousness thought. Supposedly, it helps. I don't know if it will, but here goes.

If someone finds this, hello. My name is Alexis Montclair. I'm a fairly normal woman. Well, that's not entirely true. I used to be normal. Only I wasn't. It's complicated.

I used to live in a barrage of thoughts. Every single moment of every single minute of every single day, my mind would be racing with every thought imaginable. Some would be good, some would be bad, some would be completely and totally benign to anyone and everyone. I would never have been able to do stream of consciousness writing before. There was no way my hands could keep up with my brain. I don't think that would be considered a bad thing.

I used to cry. A lot. I still do, just differently.

I have a cat. His name is Emil. He's a black and white barn cat I found in my aunt's barn three years ago. Emil was just a kitten at the time. His tiny, puff-ball body looked so cold (the mid-spring rains can be very chilling), and I felt awful for him. I scooped him up and carried him home. We've been largely inseparable ever since, though I'm not sure I'll be able to keep him. On one hand, the doctor says Emil is a calming influence on me, which I apparently need. On the other hand, my roommate/best friend, Natalie, is allergic to cats, so I think it'd be better for her health if Emil were to live somewhere else.

That doctor I mentioned isn't just one doctor, per say. I have a primary care physician, a psychologist, and a psychiatrist. They all think Emil is a great pet and a great thing to have in my life. They all provide me with the care I need. That's what I'm told. I don't know if I agree with it at all times.

There used to be wonderful, beautiful days in my life. Emil and I would lay on the apartment floor, sunbeams shining through the window onto our bodies, warming our skin and souls inside and out. I would go to work, my employer providing me with an 8 to 5 that didn't satiate my creative desires, but it did pay my bills. I worked for a fairly normal boss, Jean-Etienne was his name (he was from France, I believe). I worked at a fairly normal desk at a fairly normal building in a fairly normal part of town. Every payday, I'd go to the bar with Natalie and her sister. We'd order 2 or 3 drinks, chat about our lives for a few hours, then walk the two blocks back to the apartment. Natalie's sister would crash on the couch, while Natalie would retire to her room and I to mine. Emil liked when Natalie's sister was over. She brought cat treats.

There also used to be terribly dark and sad days in my life. Some of them were for normal reasons. Like the day I lost my job because Jean-Etienne moved his company to Europe. Or the day I got rear-ended on my way to work. Or the day we found out Natalie's sister drowned. These were all very, very bad days where I cried uncontrollably for completely justifiable reasons.

There were also very dark days where I cried and I couldn't tell you why. Most days were cheerful and wonderful -- at least 4 out of every 5 were that way. But the sad days came far too often. It was just often enough that people would tell me something wasn't right.

"You should really talk to your doctor about this. It's not right for someone to be sad like you are."

"You shouldn't cry for no reason. You're not as pretty when you don't smile."

"I'm beginning to think there's something wrong with you."

There were more, but they hurt to write. I've learned that sometimes things hurt to bring up, and that you have to take a moment to step away from them, otherwise you'll hurt worse. That's one of the things I was told would make me better. And you know what? That actually works. I'm happy something has.

The most recent doctors I visited told me I have depression and Bipolar I Disorder. I've been told a lot of things though. I've been told I have a psychosis of sorts, as well as generalized social anxiety. I've had my diagnosis changed nearly as many times as I've changed physicians. It's difficult to know who you are and what may be wrong with you when the people who are educated to know about these things can't come to a definitive conclusion themselves.

They told me I needed medication. I listened. That's what you're supposed to do when a doctor tells you that you need to do something. You listen. It's for the best for your health. Even if I didn't feel like anything was wrong, they know better. They're the experts. I'm just a girl who cries for no apparent reason as she holds her cat.

Natalie was the first person to tell me I need help. I love and hate her for it.

Two months ago, I came home crying. Natalie was in our living room, sitting on the couch watching a baseball game. She saw me and immediately gave me a hug. She hugged me until I stopped crying.

"Why were you crying, Alexis?"

"I don't know. I just cry."

I hate pills. I always have. My mother tried to get me to take vitamins as a kid, but I didn't like it. One time, she gave me a vitamin E capsule. It felt gummy on the outside, like a Gusher, so I bit into it as hard as I could, hoping it was something tasty like honey inside. It wasn't. I spit that out quicker than I've done anything else in my life.

When you're "sick" with mental illness, the doctors give you pills. I don't know why they say I'm sick though. I felt normal before. Everyone is happy, everyone is sad. No one can be just happy all the time, nor can they be just sad. Yet still, I was given pills. I crushed them up and mixed them in with my tea or hot cocoa, depending on what I was in the mood for that particular day. I didn't want to have another vitamin E incident with the things that were supposed to help me.

The good news is that I've yet to have another problem like the one I had with that exploding pill capsule. The bad news is what happened after I started taking the pills.

I've never been paranoid of anything in my entire life. Yes, I'll have moments where I'm afraid of things -- the dark, spiders, strangers on the street, bad acting -- but never to the point where I'm beyond scared about it. I've been told I'm being paranoid now though. I disagree, but that's what Natalie tells me.

I saw a gnat Monday. A single, lonely fruit fly had taken up residence in our kitchen. It lasted all of twenty minutes before Emil killed it. Damn good cat, if you ask me.

I woke up in the middle of the night, sweat pouring from my brow. They were everywhere. While I couldn't see them, I could feel them. I could feel their tiny feet. I could feel their beady little eyes watching me. Thousands upon thousands of gnats had found refuge in my apartment and were now watching me. I began to sob, loudly and painfully. It was enough to wake Natalie up in the next room. She spent the next half hour walking me through the apartment to show me there were no more bugs. She's trying so hard. I know she doesn't understand.

The next night, they were under my skin. I could feel their wings flapping as they walked up the sides of my shins, flowing back and forth between my ankles and my knees. I don't know what stopped them from moving further, but I do remember my knees hurting fiercely the entire time. It had to be that they were building a fruit fly nest in my knee. Then, when someone touched my knee next, it would explode from the pressure, like a gunshot to a cantaloupe. They'd be everywhere again. Everywhere. I just wanted them gone.

I've stayed awake the last two nights watching for them. Not just one. All of them. Emil snuggles beside me and watches at times too.

My family and friends love me. I'm trying hard -- so fucking hard -- to remember that. But if this goes on long enough, they'll stop loving me. They say they won't, but I know better.

I had a bad relationship once. Her name was Laura. We dated for just shy of a year. Not everything about it was bad. I truly think she loved me and I know that at the very least I had strong feelings for her. I'm not sure if it was love, however I realize that my opinion of that is clouded by the bias of what has happened since. After I moved out of my old apartment and in with Natalie, Laura would drive by every night, some nights more than once. There were quite a few days I saw her blue sedan sitting in the alleyway across the street. It just ran. Lights off. Exhaust fuming. But it was there. I knew she was there. She knew I knew she was there.

I'm happy for Laura now. She moved on, finding someone that she fell in love with. I know this because I ended up with a note on my window explaining that she was moving to Georgia (the state, not the country) with her new interest. The note told me that I'll miss her interest and her attention. I'm sure I have missed it, much in the same way that a person recovering from a broken leg misses the pain of a bone sticking through your flesh. I think Laura understood why I got sad. She didn't stop loving me because I got help nor because the help didn't work. She stopped loving me because she found another object of affection. You know, the way love should work.

I've become much better at hiding when I cry. If I keep it to myself, no one has to be burdened with my pain. I can cry in the same room as Natalie and she almost never notices. I think. Or maybe she's just letting me cry alone. I appreciate her either way.

Why do funerals always play classical music? When my funeral comes, I want the funeral home to play "Zula" by Phosphoresent, "One Sunday Morning" by Wilco, and "Suicide Medicine" by Rocky Votolato on repeat. Those are my songs, the ones I want there. It doesn't matter if I'm not there to hear them, it's what I would have wanted. I told this to Natalie. She suggested I add "He Films The

Clouds, Pt. 2" by Maybeshewill to the list. I'm not opposed to it, if only to make Natalie happy.

I think before the medicine I was more sensitive than most people. I think my tears were natural, strong, and passionate. I was unique. I was learning who I really was.

I'd like to think that if I were born without legs I would have found a way to succeed in the world. The same goes for if I were born without eyesight, hearing, or speech. These are merely just hurdles to climb over in order to exhibit our fullest and most beautiful potential. We go as far as our minds allow us to, no matter our physical limitations. The sky truly is the limit -- or if we're exceptionally lucky, we can climb beyond the sky and into orbit with the moon.

My rocket ship to the moon has been grounded.

I think everything is right with me. I thought that before seeking help, I think that now. I think that we all have demons we must face. I've been told mine just manifest themselves in the form of a sickness. I feel lost, not sick. I won't hurt me, I don't believe. If I were to go silent for days at a time, tens of people would notice. I'd have text message after text message wondering how I'm doing. Hell, Natalie is pounding on my door just to make sure I'm alright if I'm not awake by 10 a.m. I have a wonderful support system for this ailment.

I feel lost, not sick.

Yesterday morning, I woke up and just began crying. I tried, briefly, to stop the tears from leaving my eyes, but there was nothing I could do to stop them. I sobbed and sobbed, nearly silently in my room, rocking back and forth as I clutched one of my pillows. Emil sat on the windowsill and stared at me, likely wondering both why his owner was upset and why she hadn't gotten out of bed to feed him yet.

10 a.m. must have hit because Natalie knocked on my door, making sure I was awake.

"GO AWAY!"

"Are you okay in there, Alexis?"

"JUST GO AWAY!"

"I'm just trying to help you."

I cried harder. I'm going to drive people away. Natalie. My parents. My friends. Their friends. My doctors. Everyone. They're all going to go away. Why in the hell would anyone want to be around me? Why would anyone want to suffer through the bullshit and insanity that I bring to the table every single day? The scariest part is not whether they want to stay. I know most (if not all of them) do. Everyone is doing his or her best to put up with me.

But will I get better? Will it be soon enough? Will everyone have the otherworldly patience necessary to put up with the bullshit and the hell I bring upon them?

I used to be normal. I feel lost, not sick.

I'm an overly sensitive person in an overly

stimulating world. We're so reliant on doing everything at once for everyone that if we focus our attentions too much on any one item, we're viewed as fanatical or crazy. I'm not crazy. Someone told me the other day to get over my depression. You wouldn't say "it's just cancer" or "it's just a broken leg". Why would you say "it's just depression and you need to get over it"? It's insensitive to attack a facet of who I am because you're not comfortable with something that's part of me. Treat me like I'm normal, not like I'm an outcast.

The plus side to the pills doesn't always outweigh the side effects. With the first pills I was given, I lost 17 pounds in a three-week span. Most women would kill for that kind of weight loss result, however I just felt weak and devoid of appetite. You see, you lose a lot of weight when your body has no desire to eat anything. Literally the only thing I could keep down for half of those three weeks was water. While I'm sure that did wonders for my digestive system, as it was finally free of spicy chicken sandwiches for the first time since I was a child, it wasn't exactly the best for, you know, living. With hunger and malnutrition comes muscle pains that I couldn't even begin to explain. Imagine that your stomach is being pulled out through your spine with a serrated knife that clutches and twists every internal organ and blood vessel along the way. That might get you on the right track.

There was a set of pills that briefly caused me to eat like a maniac. I don't recall exactly why my medication was changed that time, though I have to imagine it was from the drastic weight loss of the first pills. After a few days on this new medication, I'd practically eaten myself out of house and home.

One night, Natalie ordered a large pizza and cheese bread for us to split. By the end of the evening, I'd eaten nearly all of the cheese bread and three-quarters of the pizza. That night made me feel so unhealthy that I spent the entirety of my next appointment talking my doctor into switching my medication. I'd rather starve than kill myself with obesity.

The doctors said that the mental side effects would likely be worse for me than the physical ones. While it hasn't worked out that way, I don't feel as though they lied to me. The mental side effects have sucked too. Some of them weren't that bad. The first few nights on most pills caused me to feel like my skin was two or three sizes too small on my body. It was weird, but not particularly awful.

Paranoia is a bitch. Not knowing when you're going to break down and cry isn't fun. Migraines could disappear off the face of the Earth and I wouldn't feel bad for a second. I stopped going to my weekend art class because I was convinced our instructor secretly had a knife inside his paintbrush. That knife was covered with the poison from an Amazonian tree frog. He was going to stab me right in the kidney with that knife, letting me slowly die as every last thought coursed through my mind. I never told him that. After all, before...when I was normal...I viewed him as a kind old man who reminded me of my deceased grandfather. I don't want to make my grandpa cry.

Through it all, there's been one constant. Talking helps. Yes, getting things out on paper like this helps, as does seeing my doctors, or talking to anyone about this. Natalie and I stayed up far too late last Saturday night watching a movie. I don't remember what the movie was because we just talked the whole time. We talked about her job, her upcoming trip to Minneapolis (lucky bitch), terrible relationship experiences, why Emil insists on sitting directly in front of the TV just when the movie gets good. Talking about anything other than how "sick" I am is wonderful. Everyone sees me as this hopeless statistic who can only dream to get the help I need from a healthcare system that chronically shows that it doesn't give a damn about my health. I'm not a statistic.

I feel lost, not sick.

I miss those thoughts I used to have all the time. That splendid cacophony of thoughts inside my mind competing for my attention has been silenced to the point of near extinction. I used to think about everything. I thought about how my mother and father managed to stay together all of these years in spite of their constant fighting. I thought about the absurdity of using religion and/or patriotism as a vehicle for starting a war, not to mention how nearly every war in history had one of those two items as a catalyst. I thought about how scared I was when I learned my grandpa had cancer (again). I thought about the fact that even though the only relationship I'd had in the past six years was with Laura, that I rarely felt truly alone because of the support system around me. I thought about one day finding love again, and finding someone who loves me back.

I think that's gone now. Not the love, the fear, or confusion. The emotions are all still there, albeit in a normalized (read: sedated) state. What is gone is my ability to think – and know – for myself. I used to know exactly who I was. I understood that I had a purpose in life, and that the purpose set before me was to bring goodness into the world and to help others. Life is hard. I have weaknesses. While the emotions I held before were difficult to handle and often times brought me to my last inches of sanity, I feel like a very real part of me has disappeared. I hope it's out there somewhere. I need help finding it because of the help I sought out in the first place. I need help because I got help. Odd thought, isn't it?

I don't know who I am. I don't know what I care about.

I know facts, yes. I know that my name is Alexis Judith Montclair. I know that I'm 28 years old. I know that I live in Hyde, Iowa with my cat, Emil, and my roommate, Natalie. I know that I'm an only child. I know that I'm single and unemployed, both of which are ideally temporary. I know that love running around outside in the first snowfall of the year, and I also know that my love of snow tires after Christmas passes.

I know that I love red wine and spicy chicken sandwiches, though not necessarily together. I know I'm attracted to quirky, introverted, yet personable women. I know that red hair, long, pale legs, and dark, sheer stockings will stop me in my tracks. I know that my favorite color is monarch orange (Pantone 165) and that the best time of year is any time I can wear a hooded sweatshirt that is two sizes too large. These are all undisputed and undeniable facts that have not changed in a very, very long time.

There are many things I used to think were facts, too. I used to think that I knew what it was like to be scared. I used to think that the worst pain I'd ever been through was breaking my ankle playing foursquare in the fifth grade. I used to think that everyone who was important to me would still love me the same way even if something was wrong with me. I used to think that I knew all the answers, or at the very least could come up with an answer for you. I used to think I was normal.

I feel like this has become far too complicated.

I feel like I'm going to lose my family and my friends.

I feel like I'm going to scare away Natalie and Emil.

I don't feel sick.

I feel lost.

LAMENTS OF A DISILLUSIONED TWENTY SOMETHING

At one point in time, I used to believe the world was a right and just place to live in. I blame my family for this. No amount of Hail Marys or John 3:16s will ever prepare you for life in the real world, contrary to what a small segment of the population will tell you. It's a mindful illusion meant to do nothing more than to distract from the very real problems each person encounters on a daily basis.

I'm fairly certain that with few exceptions, there is never an intent to become a selfish person. At the heart of humanity is our compassion. Without that, we are nothing more than the animals and resources we exploit (or use as our God-given right, depending on which side of the fence you fall). I know I didn't mean to become a person that looks out solely for myself and very few others. The realities of life are unavoidable.

It had to have happened sometime between the

fall of 2010 when an airport clerk in Portland sold me a half empty pack of wintergreen gum and the week in early 2013 when I watched three of my best friends lose their jobs within 48 hours of one another. Nobody in this world is there to care about you except for you. For those of you who are fortunate enough to find a true lifelong soulmate, you've got a second person coming to your aid (or so I'd hope). Realize though that you're in the minority. I found that out too late for my own good.

The "millennial" generation or Generation Y is roughly defined as those who were born between 1981 and 2004. We're an underachieving, uncaring, under motivated generation that is driving society toward a cultural bankruptcy unlike those ever seen before. That's what I've been told by individuals from previous generations who, like people from any generation, are looking to advance their own motives and goals regardless of the cost. Hell, even we millennials do it.

The problem lies in the fact that people will always play favorites and look out for their own best interests. Case in point – a young man fresh out of college came to my door the other day, résumé in hand. He wanted a job working as a systems analyst, and his degree showed that he had the right type of education for an entry-level position. I took his resume to the human resources man and the manager of the department in question, only to be told the college grad didn't have the requisite work experience for an entry-level position. How are you supposed to gain experience in a field if every employer in that field refuses to hire you due to your lack of experience?

Everyone is looking for the quickest route to the top. Whether you take the trip with the assistance of education, hard work, embezzlement, lying, cheating, stealing, sex, or some other manner entirely is a matter of ethics for each individual. However, just because someone prefers getting laid to getting good marks on a test does not necessarily mean they are any worse of a person than the latter. After all, some of the greatest scandals in American history have come at the expense of educational institutions.

Last night as I laid on my couch, petting my husky's head as he peacefully snoozed on the cushion beside me, I wondered if all my skills and talents that don't involve backstabbing someone else were all for naught. We live in a world where the greatest tool any person can have is the power of deception. Fast hands and a slick tongue are widely acclaimed resources of any industry, not just for used car salesmen, prostitutes, and magicians. The best storytellers are not the ones who can write books and make money doing it. No, the best storytellers are the ones that can make you believe in their cause enough to pay them, donate your time and money to their cause, or even vote for them.

Why shouldn't this be the method to get ahead in life? Aside from the most effective way to judge people being a true meritocracy, there's really no need to mislead people, let alone to blatantly lie to them. I had a family member once tell me that the only reason the United States won the Cold War was because it was against communism to believe in God. What the actual fuck?

If left to our own devices, I truly believe that most humans would become honest, caring, agnostic, realists who look out for themselves as well as their fellow man at every turn. Sure, it's an incredibly utopian ideal, if for no other reason than how far of a cry it is from the realities of the present. For every 500 people who are wonderful individuals that want nothing more than to be equal in the world, there's a single, solitary maniac who will use everything in their power to be sure that everything falls in their favor. These men and women become the leaders of society, business, and faith through corruption, aggressiveness, manipulation, and discord. Of course, after they get in power, we exalt their great deeds, though that's another matter altogether.

Slowly, ever so slowly, I've become one of those monsters of the world. It did not begin out of want or desire that I've turned this way, it's out of necessity. Last week, my employer came to me asking if they should hire my sister as our receptionist. My sister has been out of work for nearly a year now. While her husband is capable of providing for her and their twin daughters, if my sister were to get a job, it'd make their lives and finances immeasurably more bearable.

I told my employer the truth. My sister was unreliable. She'd been fired from her last two jobs due to attendance issues. Her attitude toward the majority of people was amicable enough, though she was a bit squeamish when talking to the elderly. Most of all, she has never shown the want to take on more work than what was detailed in her job description. My employer called her back before the end of the day to tell her that they had selected another candidate.

I felt bad to do that to my sister, but you have to fight to survive. Never let anyone catch you with your guard down. If they hired someone related to me and she didn't perform well, how would that reflect on me? Poorly at best, awful at worst. I can't have either of those adjectives attached to my name if I'm going to get ahead. It's already enough trouble to excel at a company when your name and face isn't the one on the end of people's tongues despite your work ethic. Why risk complicating matters even further?

There's no malintent meant in any of my actions. The only intent I have with any action I take is that of self-preservation. Divide and conquer. Take from the rich and become richer yourself. Don't trust anybody. These are the methods that any man or woman, myself or otherwise, must take in order to thrive and survive in the corrupted, lecherous planet that we live on. Liberal or conservative, democratized or fascist, communist or capitalist, religious or atheist, it doesn't matter what label you're fighting under, because there is a single label that unifies and destroys each and every human being.

Me.

TIA

As the dream faded, she chased it, forlorn. The dream dissolved into her mind quickly, its essence shifting from an otherworldly reality to a memory slipping further and further from her reach. With one final gasp of determination, she dove toward the final fragments of the dream within her eyesight, though she knew her efforts were futile. Her free fall seemed destined to last for an eternity.

THUD

The sound of her own body hitting the floor shocked Tia out of her slumber and into the reality of the world around her. Her eyes struggled to gather their focus in the dark room; though Tia could tell her head was inches from the foot of her bed. Tia rolled to her back in effort to better orientate to her surroundings. She caught a glimpse of her dimly illuminated alarm clock, its numerals clad in a blue hue as they mocked her from afar.

3:51 a.m....3:51 a.m....3:51 a.m....3:52 a.m....3:52 a.m.

Tia had been asleep for less than an hour when the dream -- THAT dream -- had quite literally pulled her from her slumber. It's not as though three in the morning was a normal bedtime for Tia. During her time at university, there had been a few party-filled nights where she had stumbled home at three or four in the morning, drunk and dehydrated for the entire walk. That said, prior to a month ago, it had been nearly a decade since she'd even seen three in the morning.

One month ago, more or less, was Memorial Day in the United States. It's not as though Tia could particularly keep track of time recently anyway for it to matter whether or not it was exactly a month ago. On that humid night, Tia first found herself lying in bed in the middle of the night, staring wide-eyed at her ceiling as remnants of a dream fluttered through her mind.

The dream began on a brisk, yet comfortable fall evening outside of her childhood home. Tia's feet eagerly kicked their way through red and orange maple leaves that had fallen just to the west side of the home's front porch as she made her way across the yard. Her destination was a swing set with three seats, one for her, as well as a seat each for her younger brother, Michael, and her older sister, Charlotte. Tia's father had erected the swing set for them when Tia was in kindergarten, though the last time she'd used it was sometime during Michael's middle school years. Each of the swing seats was painted in the child's favorite colors -- Michael's in blue, Charlotte's in red, and Tia's in yellow.

Tia would climb on her swing, slowly kicking her feet as a breeze swirled leaves around her. First she'd look to her left to see Michael's swing, calmly sitting still as it had been all along. Then Tia would look to her right, only to see that Charlotte had joined her. While Charlotte wore rather dark, intimidating clothing in real life, in Tia's dream she was clad in a bright pink sweatshirt with a matching baseball cap to cover her bright red hair. Charlotte's presence wasn't enough to startle Tia -- after all, Charlotte made an effort to use the swing set every time she visited their parents -- though presence would be an odd word to describe Charlotte's appearance.

Tia would try to reach out and grab Charlotte's hand, only for her hand to be just out of reach with each effort. After five or six tries, Tia would come to a quick stop on the swing, climbing off in order to stand in front of Charlotte. Tia would then attempt to start a conversation that she had with Charlotte many times in their youth.

"Do you want me to push you?" Tia would ask, her voice weak and fluttering against the strength of the autumn wind.

Instead of a verbal answer, Charlotte would bow her head, staring intently at the ground beneath her feet. She'd nod slowly, her motions executed with just enough speed for Tia to notice, though not swiftly enough for the casual onlooker to pay any heed to her movements. Tia would smile and move behind Charlotte to push her on the swing, only Charlotte would be gone.

For a few moments, Tia would turn around and around, searching for where Charlotte had run off to. At the end of her third revolution, she'd see Charlotte sprinting down the hill beside their long gravel driveway. Tia would begin to run after Charlotte, her arms stretched out with the false hope that somehow arms alone would reel Charlotte in. With each passing step, Charlotte would fade further and further into the distance, becoming smaller in Tia's sight as her arms grasped for nothing but air.

4:08   a.m....4:08   a.m....4:09   a.m....4:09 a.m....4:09 a.m.

For every minute Tia replayed the dream -- THAT dream -- in her mind, she spent another two wishing she could just stop thinking about it even existing. She'd tried everything she could think of to stop having the dream. It didn't matter what combination of alcohol, sleeping pills, boring books, or work fatigue Tia had in her system when she went to bed, the dream would make its nightly visit, playing out the exact same way every single time.

Tia pulled herself off the floor, and then guided herself to the kitchen using the edges of her walls and dresser. She peered into the fridge, her eyes temporarily blinded by the brightness of the light. In a short debate between a can of root beer and a glass of gamay wine, the soda pop won out, if only because the wine bottle reminded Tia of a bottle that Charlotte had snuck into their shared bedroom during high school. Tia shuffled her way back to bed, root beer in hand, stopping only to glare once again at her alarm clock's taunting face.

4:12 a.m....4:13 a.m....4:13 a.m....4:13 a.m....4:14 a.m.

In fewer than two hours, Tia's alarm clock would inform her that it had reached 5:55 a.m. and that if she didn't wake up right now, there was no way she'd get ready in time to go to work. With a long sigh, Tia pointed the face of the clock away from her, flipping the switches for both her primary and back up alarms off, and closed her eyes in an effort to go to sleep.

Tia awoke to the sound of her cell phone letting her know that a voicemail had just arrived. Without even checking, Tia knew exactly what the message entailed. This was her fifth day in a row not going into work. She had been fired. Not that it mattered anyway. It's not as if she'd be able to function at work on such little sleep. Listening to the voicemail would be the responsible thing to do though. Charlotte always told Tia the most responsible thing anyone could do is listen.

Tia dialed her voicemail and placed the phone on speaker. She set the phone down on her chest as the automated system began talking.

You have one new voice message and two saved messages. First message from Friday, June 24th at 10:18 a.m.

"Hello. This message is for Tia Euless. This is Amber Hardy with human resources at Anderson and Harper. I received a message this morning from your manager that you had not arrived in by 9 a.m. yet again. While we would normally look to do terminations in person, your excessive absenteeism and inability to return communication to us has left Anderson and Harper no other choice but to terminate your employment effective immediately. We will be mailing separation paperwork to your home. If you have questions about that paperwork, or if you would like to arrange for a time to pick up any personal belongings, you may call me ba..."

Message erased. First saved message from Sunday, May 29th at 11:54 a.m.

"Hey Tia. It's Charlotte. I'm sorry that I couldn't bring myself to see you today. You've always been my favorite person in the world and my biggest supporter. That's actually why I couldn't see you. I know that if I had talked to you, I would have changed my mind. You wouldn't have gone into law if you weren't convincing. I know you're probably working now, even on your day off, and I'm really sorry that I'll put a damper on your week. Just know that I love you now and I always have. You've been the best sister anyone could ever ask for. Nothing is your fault. I love you."

Message saved. Second saved message from Sunday, May 29th at 12:07 p.m.

"...Scotty. Come here Scotty. Here kitty, kitty, kitty. Where did you go? Mommy just wants to let you outside where you won't see anything. **silence** There you are! Com.. **audio becomes incomprehensible**...**silence**...**more muffled audio**...**a door slams shut** ...such a pretty cat.

123

Someone will give him a good home. ...***silence***...You will keep in perfect peace all who trust in you, all whose thoughts are fixed on you, Lord. Now take me a...**muffled audio**...fore this disease eats my body alive. Forgive me fo..."

End of message. To reply to this message, press 8. To delete this message, press 7. To save it in the archives, press 9. To hear more options, press Star. To return to the main menu, press Pound.

Are you still there? To reply to this message, press 8.

"I forgive you, Charlotte."

To delete this message, press 7.

"I love you and miss you."

To save it archives, press 9.

"You'll never be gone to me."

To hear more options, press Star.

"But I need you to go now before I join you..."

Message erased.

AN EPILOGUE TO INNOCENCE

AND THANKS GOES TO...

I don't think I ever actively set out to become an author. I've had to write papers for classes, process documents for work, minute logs for class meetings. Yet I don't think it really ever crossed my mind that I could become an author -- let alone one who has been published. It's a bit of a surreal feeling even now. There are many people whose contributions to my writing efforts cannot and should not go unrecognized, as I would not be where I am today without them.

I have to begin by thanking Erin M. for her unwavering support of my work, especially when no one else was vocally supporting me. While she certainly was not the first person to tell me that my writing was good, she was the first person to tell me that she thought my writing was good enough to get published. For that motivation and inspiration, I am eternally grateful.

I would be remiss if I did not mention the contributions of an unnamed peer reviewer, my sophomore high school English teacher, and my mother. The three of them told me that "no one will want to read a sad story", that I "wrote like a fifth grader and should consider never writing fiction again", and that "people who went to college never amounted to anything in life", respectively. Thank you all of providing me with more than enough fuel to want to prove you wrong time and time again.

I'd like to thank all of the bloggers, writers, and avid readers who took the time to peer review my book when I asked them to – or in some cases, just because they were kind enough to do so through the goodness of their own hearts. To Anna, Erin M., Erin V., Kat, Krista, Mike, Samantha, and my wife, I realize that you provided your input with little to no prompting on my part, making my work better every step of the way. I'd like to further thank Samantha for helping me re-write some portions of my dialogue that was unrealistic, Anna for unknowingly helping me realize that a couple of my stories needed to be more vivid, my wife for her extensive editing to the book during the proofing process, and Brandon and Kat for their publishing advice and expertise to help make this book possible.

I'd like to thank Ben and Jerry's for making their Half Baked ice cream, the comedy trio of Stewart, Colbert, and Oliver for providing amusement to level off the emotions writing sad stories gave me, and the alphabet for letting me borrow its letters for this book.

There have been numerous people who have offered me help/provided me help as part of the writing/publishing/promoting process. For their (sometimes intentional, sometimes not) input in those areas, a well-deserved thanks goes to Amanda C., Agent Q, Brian, Brittany, Candice, Charles, Cherie, Erin V., Eve, Janna, Karina, Kat, Kate, Katie, Kendra, Krista, Manda O., Mike, Samantha, Stephanie, Tabitha, Tim K., and my wife for their assistance in various project related endeavors. Also, since I'm writing this before the book is promoted and published, if you did something to help me out after the point at which I wrote this, thank you too.

Finally, thank you to you, the person reading this book. It's one thing to have friends, peers, or educators read your work. It's another to have a complete and total stranger read your words. It's overwhelming and wonderful all at the same time.

ABOUT THE AUTHOR

Tim Baughman Jr. is a husband, author, and blogger. He enjoys crafting letters into words, words into sentences, and sentences into stories that tug at your heartstrings with kitten eyes and melodic heartbreak. There's a statistically significant chance any pictures taken of him were quickly followed by a snarky remark.

33655968R10085

Made in the USA
Middletown, DE
22 July 2016